PRAISE FOR REBEKAH CRANE

The Infinite Pieces of Us

A *Seventeen* Best YA Book of 2018

"Crane has created an organic and dynamic friendship group. Esther's first-person narration, including her framing of existential questions as 'Complex Math Problems,' is honest and endearing. A compelling narrative about the power of friendship, faith, self-acceptance, and forgiveness."

—*Kirkus Reviews*

"Crane's latest is a breezy, voice-driven, and emotional read with a well-rounded cast of characters that walk that fine line between quirky and true to life . . . The novel stands out for its depiction of the American Southwest . . . Hand to fans of Jandy Nelson and Estelle Laure."

—*Booklist*

"[This] journey of self-discovery and new beginnings will resonate with readers seeking answers to life's big questions."

—*School Library Journal*

"*The Infinite Pieces of Us* tells a story of judgement, family, trust, identity, and new beginnings . . . a fresh take on teenage pregnancy . . . Crane creates relatable, diverse characters with varying socioeconomic backgrounds and sexualities that remind readers of the importance of getting to know people beyond the surface presentation."

—*VOYA*

The Upside of Falling Down

"[An] appealing love story that provides romantics with many swoon-worthy moments."

—*Publishers Weekly*

"Written with [an] unstoppable mix of sharp humor, detailed characters, and all-around charm, this story delivers a fresh and enticing take on first love—and one that will leave readers swooning."

—Jessica Park, author of *180 Seconds* and *Flat-Out Love*

"*The Upside of Falling Down* is a romantic new-adult celebration of all of the wild and amazing possibilities that open up when perfect plans go awry."

—*Foreword Magazine*

"Using the device of Clementine's amnesia, Crane explores themes of freedom and self-determination . . . Readers will respond to [Clementine's] testing of new waters. A light exploration of existential themes."

—*Kirkus Reviews*

"This quickly paced work will be enjoyed by teens interested in independence, love, self-discovery, and drama."

—*School Library Journal*

"First love, starting over, finding herself—the story is hopeful and romantic."

—*Denver Life*

The Odds of Loving Grover Cleveland

One of Bustle's Eight Best YA Books of December 2016

"Now that the title has captured our attention, I have even better news: No, this book isn't a history lesson about a president. Much more wonderfully, it centers on teenager Zander Osborne, who meets a boy named Grover Cleveland at a camp for at-risk youth. Together, the two and other kids who face bipolar disorder, anorexia, pathological lying, schizophrenia, and other obstacles use their group therapy sessions to break down and build themselves back up. And as Zander gets closer to Grover, she wonders if happiness is actually a possibility for her after all."

—Bustle

"The true beauty of Crane's book lies in the way she handles the ugly, painful details of real life, showing the glimmering humanity beneath the façades of even her most troubled characters . . . Crane shows, with enormous heart and wisdom, how even the unlikeliest of friendships can give us the strength we need to keep on fighting."

—RT Book Reviews

POSTCARDS
FOR A
SONGBIRD

ALSO BY REBEKAH CRANE

POSTCARDS FOR A SONGBIRD

REBEKAH CRANE

SKYSCAPE

SKYSCAPE

Published by Skyscape, New York

www.apub.com

Amazon, the Amazon logo, and Skyscape are trademarks of Amazon.com, Inc., or its affiliates.

ISBN-13: 9781542092999 (hardcover)
ISBN-10: 154209299X (hardcover)
ISBN-13: 9781542092982 (paperback)
ISBN-10: 1542092981 (paperback)

Cover illustration and design by Liz Casal

Printed in the United States of America

For you, the reader,
may this book bring you home.

This world is but a canvas to our imagination.

—Henry David Thoreau

1

BIRD ON A WIRE

When life isn't working, take another perspective. Lizzie's go-to is handstands. She flings herself against the wall and flops there like an upside-down dead fish. Somehow she manages to hold herself up. And then she usually says something like, "Imagine if we could walk upside down. Then the sky would be our playground. Wouldn't that be nice, Songbird? The sky as our playground."

And I say something like, "Wouldn't we just float around everywhere?"

"Exactly." Lizzie responds like I've asked the perfect question, even though we both know she wishes I had more of her imagination. She nods, her long brown hair dangling to the ground. Her face blooms with red, the blood rushing to her head, but she talks like she doesn't care. "We could dance on the sunrise and float to the moon."

When I tell her that her face is about to pop like a balloon, she comes down from her handstand.

"God, it feels good to be back on the earth," she says.

"I thought you wanted to dance on the sunrise."

"I realized something, being upside down."

"What?" I ask.

"Gravity is like a parent. It holds you even when you don't want it to."

Not all parents. But I keep that to myself.

When I want to take a new perspective, I prefer the top of the garage instead of a handstand. I've tried to do what Lizzie does, just fling myself upside down and trust I can hold my weight, but I always worry that I'll fall on my head. Lizzie is the only person I know who can float on clouds and dance with the sunrise, because Lizzie is made up of magical things—the stuff in the atmosphere you can't see until it lights up and becomes a shooting star.

Up on the garage, I hug my knees to my chest and perch like a bird. From here I can look around at all the rooftops in the neighborhood. Lizzie asked me once what I see from that high up. I told her most people in the neighborhood need to clean their gutters.

"That doesn't surprise me," she said.

"Why?"

"Have you seen the way some of the people walk around this neighborhood all clogged? The inside always comes out, Songbird. No matter how hard you try to ignore it."

Chief is the worst offender. His gutters are so clogged he doesn't remember what it's like to breathe without pain. Most days he's so stopped up that words get stuck in his throat and he has to force them back down with a deep swallow.

The first time Chief saw me on the roof of the garage, he asked that I "please refrain from breaking any bones or smashing my head." If Lizzie is freedom, Chief is handcuffs and locked doors.

"All it takes is one slip of the foot," he said.

"You can't live worried about slipping, Chief," I said. "Better to have the confidence you can catch yourself when it happens."

"You know that's not true, Wren. It's better to just stay away from danger. Stop talking like your sister."

I love when he compares me to Lizzie. It rarely happens.

2

"And stop calling me Chief. I'm your dad."

"OK, Chief."

His move is to put his hands on his hips, like a police officer. I'm pretty sure if you looked him up at Sacred Heart Hospital in Boise, he'd be the first recorded case of a child born with a mustache and a badge. Chief has been a police officer his entire career. He currently works the graveyard shift for the Spokane Police Department. He claims to like the action of nighttime. I think he just prefers to sleep during the day, when everyone else is awake. It keeps him properly detached from a normal life and the things people do in a normal life, like eat cereal in the morning and kiss each other before bed at night.

But I understand his choice. If all you ever see is people at their worst moments—broken, bruised, drugged, dead—humanity becomes the enemy. A thing to be tamed and tasered, not loved.

Lizzie is the one who started calling him Chief.

"Why not just call me Officer?" he asked. "Officer Plumley."

"Because it's boring," she said. "It's too long, and it doesn't sing. Don't you want your name to carry a better tune?"

"But it's accurate."

"Accuracy is overrated. I'd rather be creative. There's nothing creative in calling you Officer."

Chief's outward annoyance was really inward love. Sometimes love does that—it presents itself cloaked in something darker, in odd shapes, in tears and groans and messes, because just like the rest of us, love is afraid to be itself. Sometimes to catch love, you have to hold it to the ground, strip it down, wash the dirt away, and wait. But love will eventually surface to breathe. Most of the time.

It makes sense that Chief covers up his love. Fourteen years ago a piece of his heart walked out the door and never came back. He has to fill the hole with something. We all do.

Lizzie fills hers with stories.

Chief fills his with work.

I fill mine with blame.

Leaving does a strange thing to those who remain. It starts with one—one person who walks out the door. And a piece goes missing. But that empty space follows us, creating more holes. There was no mom to bring cupcakes to my class on my birthday in first grade, and so no one was celebrated. The day passed as any other. And more pieces went missing. The school didn't have my mom's email address, so I was left off class party lists. And a piece slips away. A school play. A science fair. Empty chairs where a mom would have sat and cheered. Until one day in junior high school, I was forgotten. I became like vapor—barely felt and rarely seen.

But Lizzie kept me from being lonely.

Love made Lizzie, but by the time I came around, it was practically gone from our house. All that was left were ghosts and the faint echo of what once was. I was made from discarded scraps of love—the pieces left out in the rain, like a rusted lawn chair someone brings inside for just one night, hoping it will salvage the whole house.

But people leave anyway, because small scraps of love, left unsown, blow away easily in the wind. And yet the rusty, weighted chair remains.

Some people are just born different. But not an intriguing different. A lonely different. An invisible different. A forgotten different. Even my mom knew it. Chief won't admit it, but I'm sure I'm the reason she left. I'm the piece that broke it all.

When life isn't working, take another perspective. Life on the ground hasn't been so good lately. Chief doesn't want me on the roof, but it's what birds do. We balance ourselves on the tiniest wires, and when the wind blows, we see if we can stay steady. You'd think we'd learn our lesson and find a more stable place to sit and watch the world below, but I see more birds on wires than anywhere else. It's in our nature. We're drawn to the edge.

And even when birds seem to be falling toward the ground, somehow we catch ourselves before we hit the pavement. Right before we lose it all, we find the strength to soar skyward again.

2

POLAR OPPOSITES

Let's get one thing clear: everyone is pretending. Life is so much easier when imagined. For example, right now Chief and I are pretending that it's six thirty at night and not eight in the morning. And that's not the only thing.

"What are you doing?" Chief says, addressing the *Wheel of Fortune* contestant skeptically. Then he solves the puzzle, saying each word loudly at the television, overly enunciating, his beer cupped in his hand, the condensation dripping on the couch. "Baking a turkey potpie."

"*Making* a turkey potpie," I correct him.

On the TV the contestant is enthusiastic. "Pat, I'd like to solve the puzzle."

And Pat Sajak, who's pretending to be a deep shade of carrot orange when really it's a spray tan, says, "OK, Rita, go for it."

Pat's aura is a pickle green. I can see it through the television. It clashes with the orange.

As loudly as Chief had been a moment ago, contestant Rita says, "Making a turkey potpie!"

If only people were as easy to solve as the puzzles on *Wheel of Fortune*.

I was right, and Chief gives me a sideways grin as if he doesn't know whether to smile at this moment or frown because there's something depressing about watching a DVRed episode of *Wheel of Fortune* at eight in the morning while drinking light beer. I'm sure it's the same at six thirty every night at the Spokane Happy Homes Assisted Living Center. Ida, Virginia, and Dolores probably get together in the common room and comment on Vanna White's dress and Pat Sajak's bad tan, yelling "Big money! Big money!" and drinking sherry. And in both places people are just surviving, but no one wants to admit it.

"Phrase," I say at the beginning of the next round, echoing Pat, my eyes on the TV.

"Wren," Chief says, setting his beer down on the coffee table.

"It's a prize puzzle, so it's probably something to do with the beach. They always send people to warm places."

"We need to talk."

This is the moment Chief decides to stop pretending.

He's on his third beer. He just got home from working the graveyard shift. Chief barely remembers what it's like to live in a world dictated not by the light of a siren but by the warmth of sunshine. I shouldn't blame him for his lack of imagination. His aura is smoke gray, like the color of murky twilight right before everything goes dark.

I've felt it brewing, like I've felt summer creeping in and drying the usually humid spring air. Chief is turning, just like the seasons. I prefer waiting. Change means moving on, and I'm not ready for that. Chief and I need to hold still for a while longer.

I get another beer from the fridge and replace his empty one. Chief drinks six beers every day—no more, no less. He figured out years ago that six was enough to put him to sleep so that whatever he saw last night at work doesn't haunt him. At least, not while he's awake. I can't speak for his dreams.

Fourteen years ago, when he woke up and discovered he was a single dad, Chief decided that the only way to stay sane was regimen. That's how we get through life. Lizzie hated it. She spent fourteen years messing everything up.

And yet, presently, the house is too clean.

"Thanks," Chief says when I set the beer down on the table.

"What's my gesture?" I ask.

"Huh?" He looks extra tired today, which means something bad probably happened last night. Rarely is it death. But I think seeing people who are willing to live desperately is worse. We're all clinging tightly to life, but at night Chief sees people holding on by a thread, their nails bloody, their fingers bruised, their hearts barely beating in the dark.

"If you were to classify me as a gesture, what would it be?" I ask. "Am I a smile? A frown? Please don't tell me I'm a furrowed brow."

"A furrowed brow?"

"Yeah, a furrowed brow." I imitate it. "You're clearly 'hands on the hips.'"

"I'm confused as to what you're asking me," Chief says.

I point at him. "Right now you're furrowing your brow. Maybe I'm wrong about you."

Chief stands up and places his hands on his hips. "You're trying to distract me."

"No, I just think I'm a furrowed brow, and I want your opinion," I say. Chief looks at me, bags under his eyes and sallow skin and gray hair that wishes it was brown again. And I wish I were a hug. A freaking gigantic "Great-Aunt Evelyn who smells like Chanel Number 5 and has smooshy boobs the size of melons" hug. The kind of hug a person disappears into and never cares to come out of. Love that people dissolve into. Love that people need.

"You've barely left the house in a month," he says.

"It rained all last week."

7

"You never see anyone."

"People are overrated. You say that all the time."

"I saw you on the roof again," Chief states, his tone hardening.

"You named me Wren. You shouldn't be surprised that I act like a bird."

"I actually wanted to name you Joan."

"Only a person whose gesture is 'hands on the hips' would name someone Joan."

"Come on, Wren."

"You can call me Joan if you want to. Will that make you feel better?"

"No, I like you as Wren. And this isn't about me." Chief takes a sip of his beer. The sip turns into a gulp that turns into a burp. He pounds his chest, trying to unclog himself, but we both know it's not that easy.

On *Wheel of Fortune*, contestant Rita solves the prize puzzle: "Meet me at the swimming pool!" Both Chief and I get distracted as Pat tells Rita she's won an all-inclusive cruise to the Dominican Republic.

"I was right. She won a trip someplace warm." I point at the TV. "Would you ever want to go on a cruise?"

"No," Chief says in his always practical voice. "I have no desire to be locked on a vessel in the middle of the ocean with hundreds of strangers. You're guaranteed to get food poisoning or the mumps."

"If you could go anywhere in the world, where would you go?"

"Stop trying to distract me, Wren."

"I'm not," I say, even though I totally am. My stomach churns with the unease felt right before you know something is about to push you over the edge. Chief is nudging me toward a cliff.

"You're alone too much," he says.

"Teenagers are allowed to be alone. And I have Olga."

"Come on," Chief says. "A dog would be more interactive than Olga."

"Then let's get a dog. I'm fine with that." Olga is the woman who stays at our house overnight when Chief works the graveyard shift. Her job sounds easy. She just needs to sleep and keep us safe, but even Olga messes up.

"I think you should go live with your aunt Betsy in Utah."

Reality check—Aunt Betsy has five children. We spent Christmas in Utah three years ago, and I still wake up with nightmares of her kids' earsplitting cries. It's like being shell-shocked.

"She's a good mom," Chief says. "You'd have more people around. It would be a better life."

"A better life?"

"You would have *a* life."

"I have a life."

"Do you?"

I don't know why Chief has decided to do this today of all days. Maybe he saw someone battered and bullied last night and it's still in his system. Those things have to pass through us, like oxygen, circulating in the veins, touching each extremity until the body knows it everywhere. Only then can the memory be exhaled.

"You don't think she's coming home," I state.

"I didn't say that."

He didn't have to. I focus my attention on the television as Rita celebrates solving another toss-up puzzle.

Chief takes a long gulp of his beer, and then his body heaves a much-needed sigh. "It's been a month."

As if I don't know that. As if I don't wear the days wrapped around my neck, each one heavier and heavier.

"Wren," Chief says.

"Don't say it."

She might never come back. Those are the words Chief is about to utter.

I ask again, "What's my gesture, Chief?"

9

Neither of us will look at each other. All focus is on the TV.

"I don't like this game," he says. "Let's stick with puzzles we can solve."

Chief finishes his beer and places the empty can on the table. Rita makes it to the bonus round, and Chief and I resume yelling at the TV. There's no more talk of Utah. It's so much easier to watch other people win or lose.

Rita has ten seconds to solve the final puzzle. We watch intently.

With one second left, she exclaims, "Polar opposites!"

She wins a car.

I bring Chief another beer, and we settle back into our comfortable nook of morning detachment. It might be more like a ravine, like a place Chief and I are stuck in, but there's comfort in knowing there's no way out. We can't leave, so we make a home in the dark, sit back, and watch *Wheel of Fortune*. It wasn't always like this, but there's a vacant room in our house. The old footprints Lizzie left on the carpet no longer exist. The echo of leaving lives here now, cavernous and cold. Chief and I have taken up residency in the emptiness, waiting for the light to come back to us.

Some of us are just better at pretending life is all right.

"I think there's something going on at the house next door," Chief says. "Just be aware."

"OK, Chief."

He knows I'm blowing off his warning. It's a habit I'm guessing most kids raised by police officers have. Some days I'm pretty sure Chief believes nothing is safe.

"I'll keep an eye out," I add, which relaxes him a little.

"What about you?" he asks. "If you could go anywhere in the world, where would you go, Wren?"

"Nowhere," I say. "I want to stay right here."

3

HOPE THROUGH THE TREES

I painted Lizzie a forest on her walls. She said it was the only way she could sleep. Lizzie has always been restless.

"My feet just want to wander, Songbird. Even at night. Even in the dark. Why would God give us legs if she didn't want us to ramble?"

Lizzie never stopped. She was a rolling stone, just like our mom. We all knew it, even from an early age. She never pretended to be any different. That's why Chief wasn't surprised when she left.

But me . . . I had to do something to help stop her leaving. It may have been selfish and hopeless in the end, but no matter how many times people leave me, I still beg them to stay, even if I'm just grasping at the wind.

It started as one tree, with emerald leaves and walnut branches, but there's loneliness in one, and I couldn't have Lizzie lonely. She needed more.

"Paint me a forest, Songbird," Lizzie said. "A place we can hide. Wouldn't that be great?"

Chief let me do it, because it drove Chief crazy that Lizzie was the worst sleeper. He'd tell stories about her as a child—how she never napped, how she only ever slept four hours at night, how she had night terrors, how when she came out of the womb, she looked around at the doctors and nurses—and even at our mom—and focused really hard, which is odd for a baby, because usually they're born all googly eyed. But not Lizzie. She was observant. She knew she had arrived, and she was ready to start living.

"From the beginning she wanted more," Chief said.

When I asked Chief what I was like as a baby, he said I was a relief. I was so boring it was nice.

"You slept. You ate. If I left the room and came back, you stayed in exactly the place I left you. At times I'd forget you were even there." Then he pointed at Lizzie. "But that one. She drove me crazy. She would disappear on me the moment I turned my back."

That's how Lizzie broke her leg when she was little. Chief went to take a quick shower, leaving Lizzie and me in front of an episode of *Sesame Street*, and the next thing he knew, Lizzie was at the bottom of the basement stairs, her leg twisted up and the bone popping out. But me . . . I was still sitting on the couch exactly where Chief had left me. At least, that's what he says. I was too little to remember.

But I could tell that a part of Chief liked that Lizzie made him work so hard. If he had wanted a desk job, he'd be an accountant.

Chief said Lizzie was searching for love from the second she drew her first breath. The moment our mom left and love disappeared, Lizzie was determined to find it again. Once she caught a glimpse of what the world could offer, Lizzie wanted it.

So I painted the trees. And after the trees, I made flowers. And after the flowers, I added butterflies and grass and a moon and clouds until the entire universe was painted on Lizzie's walls, and she could wander the earth at night, searching for love, and fall asleep under the stars.

But no matter how many trees I painted, I was still afraid she'd leave me.

Chief knew Lizzie wouldn't find what she was looking for in the forest I created, but I couldn't paint our mom on the walls. I don't even know what she looks like.

"Wren, where do you think she is today?" Lizzie asked me once as she stood on her hands upside down in her room. It looked like she was swinging from one of my trees, her knees bent and wrapped around a branch, her brown hair falling toward the floor like a waterfall.

"I don't care," I said, sitting with my knees pulled into my chest.

"Your black hair matches the night sky," Lizzie said. "And your green eyes match my trees. You're all around me, Songbird."

She was buttering me up. Lizzie knew I loved when she talked in colors. She's the only person I've told about my ability to see auras. I'm weird enough as it is, but Lizzie never made me feel that way.

"Come on, just play along," she said. "You're good at this."

"No, I'm not."

"Maybe she's a chalk artist in Paris."

"I'm not doing this." I tried to make myself into a tiny ball.

"Don't hold your wings in so tightly. How are you ever going to fly?" Lizzie asked.

But I didn't want to fly. I wanted to stay exactly where I was, with Lizzie.

"How about working for UNICEF, vaccinating children all over the world?" Lizzie's voice was strained from the pressure of being upside down. That's the thing with handstands—a person can't stay like that forever. There's something poetic about only being able to dance on the sunrise and float on the moon for a small time. Poetic some days, depressing others.

"Come down from that tree," I said. "You're going to hurt yourself."

"Not until you play along, Songbird."

"But she can't administer vaccines. No medical skills and she hates blood."

"Running a communist boot camp somewhere in Poland, with Stalin's great-granddaughter, whose name is Anastasia, and wearing one of those big furry hats."

"Wherever Mom is, it isn't here!" In my anger, the tiny ball I was attempting to be cracked, and I exploded all over Lizzie's floor, flopping onto my back and spreading out like a dead jellyfish.

Lizzie just stayed upside down. She would risk brain damage to make me happy. "Songbird," she said calmly, "it doesn't hurt to pretend. You can either have tentacles as arms, or wings. You decide."

The world could be anything when I was with Lizzie. She pulled the stars down from the sky and held them in her hands.

I sat up, my arms lighter and dangling at my side.

"OK," I said. "Singer in a vaudeville-style show somewhere in Croatia, where she plays a life-sized marionette with painted red cheeks and sings a song called 'Some Strings Are Meant to Be Broken.'"

Lizzie set her feet down and grinned widely. When all the blood left her face, she looked even more radiant. "And dances in point-shoes," she said.

"It's the best number in the show."

We lay down and gazed up at the universe I'd painted on her ceiling.

"She has a cat named Greta Garbo that drinks champagne instead of milk," Lizzie said.

"And she signs autographs every night." I felt like we were floating on clouds instead of lying on old carpet. Possibility can make you weightless.

"It's no wonder Mom can't be here with us," Lizzie said. "What would the show do without her?"

"And Greta Garbo? Cats can't open champagne bottles by themselves."

"Mom *can't* come home. It wouldn't be fair. The show and Greta Garbo depend on her. They need her." Then Lizzie whispered, "See, I told you it wouldn't hurt. Isn't life better when it feels extraordinary, Songbird?"

I wish extraordinary lasted, but it never does.

"Tell me again what my aura is," she said.

"Cadmium yellow."

"The color of the sun." Lizzie smiled.

Lizzie didn't need me to paint daylight on her walls. She *is* light. I painted a nightscape instead, because she always had trouble at night. One time, I found her in her room, shaking from a nightmare, and Lizzie said she was trapped.

"Will you sing to me, Songbird?"

And so I did.

I thought if I gave her painted stars and a moon and trees she knew as well as she knew herself—a fixed night with nothing to scare her—Lizzie wouldn't be so afraid of the dark.

"Will everyone leave me behind?" I asked that day on the floor of Lizzie's room, when we imagined our life as extraordinary. "No one wants to remember a broken heart."

She grabbed my hand and said, "The trees will remember you. They're not going anywhere. You can build a nest in them, Songbird, if you want."

Lizzie promised me the trees would stay, but she never promised that she would.

When I stand in Lizzie's room, her walls like the dense, dark forest around Spokane, I know why Chief let me paint all of this. He knew Lizzie wanted to get lost. She wanted to disappear, even if only in her imagination, even if only when she was in her room. Chief and I hoped that if she could get lost in her own bedroom, we could keep her safe and maybe Lizzie wouldn't go searching beyond the walls of our house.

It's been thirty-two days since she left.

4

ANNE BOLEYN

I'm lying in the grass, thinking about how Claude Monet used only nine colors when he painted. He knew what he liked. Why clog up his life with unnecessary shades? Anyone can paint a universe with just three colors.

Monet was a genius.

I'm also pretending I can't hear Chloe's mom talking about me. It's not working. Some voices demand to be heard. Her aura is tiger orange—not everyone can wear her, but everyone takes notice when she's around.

Chloe's mom is one of those people who constantly contradicts herself in the same breath and then blames other people for it.

I never lie, but if you're looking to me for the truth, you won't get it.

I promised myself I'd never say this, but since you're asking . . .

Right now she's saying, "I pride myself on not butting into *any* other family's business, but I warned him this might happen if he didn't get that girl under control. I told him so myself, even though I swore I never would."

Another cop wife says, "What about the other one?"

"Wren?" Chloe's mom says. "She's harmless. She'll never leave. Most of the time I forget she's there."

Chloe's mom is like the tuna casserole Chief brings to the Spokane police force's weekly softball match in Manito Park. On the outside it's put together and presented nicely, but the inside stinks and might give you food poisoning. No one eats it, and yet we keep bringing the casserole because it's the only potluck dish Chief knows how to make. It's part of the routine.

That's how I feel about Chloe's family. They're Chief's six beers, the grocery list he gives me every Sunday, the uniform he wears, *Wheel of Fortune* every morning at eight. Chloe's family is just a part of our routine. They're the only dish we know how to make, and instead of looking up a new recipe, we risk food poisoning, because a new recipe is a gamble. It might be a mess. It might taste like hell. It could be a disaster, and we can't have another one of those.

This might be why Monet used only nine colors. He knew what made him comfortable, but even Monet ditched ivory black after 1886.

I close my eyes and let the sun heat my eyelids until they burn. I think I might be able to disintegrate right here in the grass. Slowly my body will be overtaken by blades of pine green and then swallowed by the warm chocolate brown of the earth, until I'm pulled so far from the surface, even the imprint of my body on the grass will disappear.

But before that can happen, a shadow hangs over me, cooling the air like a cloud blocking the sun, but it isn't a passing cloud. It's a blanketing storm.

"I didn't think you were coming." These are the first words Chloe has said to me in a month. In the endless bank of possibilities, this seems uncreative.

How are you holding up since the sun disappeared? Can I warm you up with friendship?

Do you need me to help rebuild your nest? I'm good at collecting sticks and feathers.

Can I hold your hand and keep you safe?

That would have been nice.

I shouldn't be surprised. Chloe's aura is red, candy-apple red. Covered in sweetness on the outside, tart on the inside.

She's been extra tart since she started making out with Jay Jameson in the hallway after English class.

High school is like dating Henry VIII. You know it's fat, with a bad case of gout, and yet you're forced to think it's sexy. You're forced to hope and dream and wish that ugly, misogynistic Henry VIII might pick you to dance with while he eats a gigantic chicken thigh and exhales bad breath on you, because he's Henry the freaking VIII and he rules the world. But the second Henry doesn't want you anymore, you're off to the guillotine.

Chloe is Anne Boleyn, and right now she's sitting on a throne she doesn't believe will crumble. Chloe thinks she rules the world. But I know how this ends. History doesn't change.

Lizzie never liked Chloe.

"What's her aura, Songbird?" Lizzie asked years ago, when I first told her that people have auras, but not the hippie kind that change based on mood or if the moon is in the Seventh House. Auras that cling to them, surround them, hold them together. With my black hair and green eyes, I'm a walking color palette, and so is everyone else.

When I said candy-apple red, Lizzie shook her head. "Be careful with her."

"Why?"

"That kind of red is selfish," Lizzie said. "It demands attention."

I got upset. Chloe was my only friend, and if I lost her, I'd have no one to spend time with when Lizzie wasn't around. After all, Lizzie likes attention, too. She's the freaking sun—cadmium yellow demands devotion. She blazes and warms and heats the universe. But Lizzie said some people want attention because they need to see the truth. They shine a light. Others like attention so they can lie, manipulate, and bend the world to their liking.

I sit up on my elbows, look up at Chloe hovering over me, and say, "Chief threatened to send me to Utah if I didn't leave the house."

"I hear there's good skiing in Utah."

Chloe and her mom came over after Lizzie left.

I perched on the roof, knees hugged to my chest, while Chloe stood in the driveway.

"Chief wants me to tell you to come down," she said.

I didn't respond. There were no words worth saying.

Chloe spoke louder. "You've been up there for a day. You're gonna hurt yourself. Come down right now, Wren."

She has always been demanding. And most of the time I follow, but not anymore. It was impossible to hurt more than I did at that moment. Her logic wasn't persuading me.

"What are you thinking? You're acting crazy!"

I wasn't thinking. In my head a picture replayed of a bird I saw once. It was pouring rain—the kind that comes down in wavy sheets in Spokane in the spring and fall. Rain that claims its territory. There is no place outside to hide in that kind of rain. Nothing can save you from getting drenched. I was huddled in a Dollar Tree when the clouds overflowed. Surrounded by the smell of cheap plastic and angry people hoping to find happiness in items that break easily.

I stood at the window and stared at a bird stuck in the storm.

The wind blew, and the rain poured, and this wide-winged bird looked frozen in the middle of it all. It was floating in midair, caught off guard by the sudden change nature decided to unleash. Held still by the fierce weather. The bird was perched on nothing. It was lost in the storm. Maybe it had a safe nest in a tree or a lookout under a bridge somewhere close, but that day, getting there was impossible. Life had changed too quickly, and all this bird could do was wait and make itself one with the storm.

"Fine!" Chloe yelled when I wouldn't come down from my perch on the roof. "You're gonna fall and hurt yourself. Don't say I didn't warn you!"

Seeing Chloe now, I haven't missed her.

"Still dating Jay?" I ask, even though I know she is from her Instagram posts. Yesterday she posted a picture of her bikini-clad body at the pool.

> **@chloethequeen** Just getting a tan and drinking slushies at the pool. #tantime #myboyfriendisalifeguard #bestsummerever #brainfreeze

"I know you don't like him, but you just don't know him like I do. He's a good guy."

Said every woman who married Henry VIII.

"You just don't understand what it's like to have a boyfriend, because you've never had one."

At that I get up and walk away. I wouldn't even be here if Chief hadn't threatened to move me to a place with too much sunshine and God.

I get a plate at the potluck table and start filling it with macaroni salad and chips, even though I have zero intention of eating. Chief's tuna casserole sits untouched.

Chloe's mom approaches me and grabs my face in her hands. "Wren, dear, it's good to see you." Mrs. Dillingham examines me further. "You look pale. Chloe's been at the pool a lot lately. Why don't you tag along with her? Get some sun."

If sunshine was that easily caught, Lizzie would already be back.

"She burns too easily," Chloe says.

"Well, why don't you take Wren with you tonight."

"What?" Chloe barks.

"You're going out with Jay." Then Mrs. Dillingham whispers to another cop mom excitedly, like we can't all hear. "Chloe has a boyfriend. And he is *so* cute!"

"Mom." Chloe demands her attention. "I'm sure Wren doesn't want to go."

At that moment, Chief runs up to the potluck table, sweating, baseball mitt still on his left hand. When he's not in the field, he's the designated umpire, a clipboard of the Spokane Recreational Softball rules never far from his reach.

"Wren doesn't want to go where?" he asks.

"Chloe's going out with her boyfriend," Mrs. Dillingham says. "I think Wren should tag along."

"She'll be a third wheel," Chloe says curtly, and then amends her statement to be sweeter. "I don't want Wren to feel left out. That's all. She'd be bored."

There's the candy-apple red I know so well.

"Well, I'm not going to tell you what to do," Mrs. Dillingham trills, "but I think you should take Wren with you."

Chief gives me a look that says *UTAH*. I have no argument. Chloe has no argument. And it's settled. Chloe and I leave the softball game as if we're still best friends, even though I'm pretty sure I was more of a *convenient* friend all these years. I have always been Chloe's trusted old teddy bear that she can hug when she needs comfort and leave behind when she's feeling grown.

The moment we get to her car, Chloe tells me she's not taking me with her.

"Look, I like Jay. I can't have you ruining this for me."

I can practically see Chloe's head dropping into a basket.

21

I tell her fine. I don't want to go anyway. This was always inevitable. I'm not surprised by her leaving, only surprised by my own naïveté.

Chloe doesn't offer to take me home, so I walk.

It's dusk. The streetlights around our neighborhood illuminate the dimness of the evening, and I think I know why Monet stopped using ivory black. There's enough darkness in the world. He knew better than to add to it.

5

A LIGHT IN THE ATTIC

A light comes on in the house next door. Outside it's dark. Down the hallway a forest lies empty. In my room I lie staring at the ceiling. Covered in nighttime, I wait to hear the familiar sounds of Lizzie, but I catch only the echo of our old wooden floors heaving in the summer heat.

When the light comes, illuminating the bedroom window directly across from mine, I'm caught off guard. Chief had said he thought something was going on next door.

I watch from my window and eventually see a boy move around the room. This late at night, it feels like we're the only two people awake in all of Spokane.

Maybe that's why I decide to turn on my bedroom light, too.

Then he comes to stand framed by the window across from mine.

He has red hair, but not carrot red, darker than that. Garnet red, and gingerbread-brown eyes, a map of freckles across the bridge of his nose that could be constellations. Even from this distance, I can see all these details.

But then I notice his lack of an aura. He's haloed in space. Just like me. Blank.

There's a reason my room is white—white walls, white bed, white furniture. It's so a person can't see the spaces left from all the leaving. The reminders of what was. The holes torn in the space that is my life. When a person is nothing, she's practically invisible.

Is he the same?

I can't take my eyes off him.

He holds up a phone and mimics typing.

What's your number? he mouths.

I write it on a sheet of paper and hold it up so he can read it.

Shortly after, a text rings through to my phone from an unknown number.

U look sad

I glance at my reflection in the mirror. Is this the face of a person who is sad? The word feels too small to suffice.

I glance back at him and shrug.

That's when he presses his lips to the window and blows so hard it vibrates and makes a loud farting sound I can hear all the way at my house.

I laugh for the first time in over a month.

He smiles.

Another text rings through to my phone.

I'm Wilder

When I look back at his window, the light is off, and the boy with the universe sprinkled across his nose is gone.

6

THE PROBLEM WITH BEES

Our old Radio Flyer wagon is parked outside Rosario's Market, the small grocery store just down the street from my house. Lizzie and I have been in charge of the grocery shopping since she started high school. It was Chief's effort to give her "responsibility." Rosario's is one of those old-fashioned markets with overpriced food and premade meals and a mechanical pony out front to entertain complaining toddlers for a penny. Lizzie eyed the horse every week.

"Check it out, Songbird. Freedom costs only a penny."

"It's a fake horse," I said. "It won't take you anywhere."

"You know as well as I do that 'freedom' is a noun, not a verb. People always think they're stuck, but people carelessly lose freedom when it falls out of their pockets and gets lost in couch cushions. If only people knew how precious pennies really are."

I started a penny collection after that, but I never told Lizzie. I'd been storing them in a big mason jar in my closet, waiting until it was overflowing with freedom before I gave it to her. Now freedom might remain hidden indefinitely under old clothes that no longer fit.

I pass the pony, its fake eyes taunting me, and walk into the market, Chief's grocery list in hand. He makes one every week, with the same items. Even the pony seems to know I'm missing something. Like it needs to remind me.

This morning as we watched *Wheel of Fortune*, Chief handed me the list and said, "Time to get back out there."

"Where?"

"Into the real world."

"What do you call this?" I gestured to our real house and our real furniture.

"You know what I mean, Wren." His expression reminded me that Utah is a real place, too. Tonight he goes back on the graveyard shift after a few days off, which means today he naps and Olga, the woman who sleeps at our house while Chief works, will stay on the couch. Chief always looks a little relieved when he knows he gets to live in darkness again.

"And you start Driver's Ed tomorrow," he said.

I was hoping he'd forget about that.

"You need to learn to drive, Wren."

He's probably right. Chief made me get my permit when I turned sixteen a few months ago, but I have yet to put it to use. Once school starts, I might be the last junior at South Hill High School without a license.

"You have a car waiting for you if you'd just learn to drive it."

An old police cruiser sits in the driveway, without the labels and sirens and the cage that's usually in the back for criminals. Chief bought it from the department ten years ago for $1,000 so Lizzie and I could have a car to drive when we turned sixteen.

When we were in junior high, Lizzie and I would sit in the front seats, me pretending to drive and Lizzie as passenger. Lizzie never wanted to drive. She hated it. Her eyes wanted to catch everything, to drink it all in and spin her imagination around reality until the world became more than just prescribed roads and stop signs.

"It makes me dizzy, Songbird. Everything moves so fast. It's too . . . sad. I just want to slow down and walk. We can't see anything clearly from a moving car."

She would hang her arm out the window and grab the air, holding a piece of the invisible in her hand.

But most days, we'd sit in the cruiser just pretending it was moving, a portion of Lizzie's body—whether it be her feet or her arm—always hanging half-out of the car's open window, gently dangling in the wind. Behind the wheel, I felt rigid and responsible. At times I'd even find myself grasping the steering wheel and checking the rearview mirrors, just to be safe. We all have our roles.

Lizzie's favorite thing to do was imagine the criminals who once sat in the back of the cruiser.

"Chief says most criminals are on drugs," I said.

"That's just their crime, Songbird." Lizzie looked into the back seat like it was filled with the spirits of criminals past. "That's not the real story."

"What's the story, then?"

"Love," Lizzie said. "Little pieces of broken hearts are littered back there. Can't you see them?"

I looked closer, but "real" to Lizzie never meant fact. Truth was a ghost, and Lizzie was a medium—she saw what no one else could.

"That's the real story why people do drugs, Songbird. You can't really live without complete, full love, and so you fill the space with medicine to hold your heart together."

Lizzie made drug addicts sound beautiful, whereas Chief painted them as dangerous. I didn't know what to think. Sometimes beautiful and dangerous go together.

"*I'm* made of rusted, unwanted pieces," I said. "Do I belong back there?"

But Lizzie just put the seat back and said, "Open the sunroof, Songbird. I want to kiss the sky."

She never did acquire a license, and I was thankful, thinking that might mean she'd stay. But in the end it didn't matter. All she needed were her two legs to leave.

I'm different. Chief knows it. That's why he signed me up for Driver's Ed.

I didn't tell him what I was thinking—that I don't want to drive the cruiser alone. That every time I sit in the front seat, I'll look to my right and see Lizzie sitting there, arm hanging out the window, long brown hair catching the wind. Radiant, before she dissolves into nothing and the world goes cold again.

"If you get your license, you won't have to drag the wagon to the grocery store anymore," Chief said. "It'll make life so much easier."

That's what he thinks. Chief has always lacked imagination.

When *Wheel of Fortune* ended, Chief said, "How about I get the art supplies out of the basement for you? It'll feel good to paint something."

But I'm not ready for that.

"It's Sunday, Chief," I said. "I'll stick to the grocery list."

Now at the grocery store, I'm reaching for a bag of Cheetos from the shelf, when someone says, "Don't get that."

Next to me a girl is stocking potato chips. Her hair is black, pulled into two buns that sprout from the top of her head.

"What?"

She looks at me and says, in a hushed tone, like she's sharing a secret, "Don't get that."

"Why not?"

"Three words." The girl leans in closer. "Yellow Number Six." I give her a confused look, and she continues. "Artificial coloring. That shit contains carcinogens."

I look at the bag. "It does?"

She examines the other items in my basket. Her face falls in disappointment.

"Artificial colors. Genetically modified. Synthetic rice fillers. *Soy.* Are you looking to get cancer?" she asks.

"Not particularly."

"Don't get this garbage."

"I don't have a choice. It's on the list." I show her Chief's well-written column of items.

"That list is killing you. Throw it away."

"I wish it was that simple," I say. "It's not my list. It's my dad's."

The girl gives me a knowing look. "I get it. My dad's a pharmacist. He thinks there's a pill to cure everything. I'm Leia Gonzalez, by the way. Like the princess."

"Wren Plumley," I say. "Like the bird."

Leia's body might be small, but her turquoise-blue aura radiates all around her, making her golden-brown skin practically shimmer. She's vibrant life captured in a tiny package.

"Did you just start working here?" I ask.

"No," Leia says. "I've been here about a year."

I don't ever remember seeing her, which seems impossible, considering how vivid she is. But in the past, I spent most of my time trying to keep Lizzie focused and on task. There was no time to look around. I never noticed much but her, the pony, and Chief's list.

"You go to South Hill High, right?" Leia asks.

"Yeah."

"I've seen you around."

"You have?"

Leia nods. "I'll be a senior next year."

"Junior," I say, awestruck.

I can't stop staring, slightly suspicious. *No one* notices me.

Leia's wearing a red apron with one pin on it—**SAVE THE BEES.** I point to it. "What's that about?"

She turns serious. "China is cutting honey with synthetic rice fillers and pumping bees with lethal antibiotics. It's a mess."

"Wow."

"If we can't trust our honey, what can we trust?"

"I guess I'll *bee* careful."

Leia laughs. Then she takes a bottle out of her pocket and dabs oil on her wrists.

"Patchouli oil," she says. "It's a natural antidepressant. My parents wanted to put me on meds, but I was like, *No way in hell.* I won't let society manipulate me. Doctors just want to give people a Prozac bandage, but guess what?"

"What?"

"That bandage leads to more bandages, and suddenly you're not only taking a pill for depression; you're taking a pill because your depression pill causes constipation. And now you're not just emotionally clogged, but literally clogged. But you know what the side effects of patchouli are?"

"Smelling like dirt?"

Leia laughs again. "I'd rather smell like dirt than be clogged with shit."

"Amen," I say. "So . . . where do I get some of that oil?"

Leia takes me by the arm, leading me toward another aisle. "Let me give you a little education on genetically modified food . . ."

But as we're turning the corner, a streak of bright, blinding light almost knocks me over.

For a moment I stumble, unable to see anything, but hands grab me quickly and place me back on my feet. I hear Leia say, "You're not supposed to ride your board in the store, Luca. You're gonna get fired."

"Wouldn't be the first time," he says. It was *his* hands that stopped me from falling.

"You can't get fired. You just got this job."

My vision starts to adjust to the light. A boy stands in front of me, though his features are still blurred slightly. I know it's all in my head. I try to act normal, like I'm not completely freaking out, but normal has never been easy for me.

"Nothing in life is permanent," he says.

"But in a sea of artificial flavors and hormone-injected meat, you make working here better, so get rid of the damn board, or I'll kick your ass." Leia shoves him in the shoulder.

"OK, don't hurt me, Princess," Luca says. "I won't skateboard in the store anymore."

He kicks his skateboard into the air and catches it effortlessly. And I know I'm looking at him with this pinched expression on my face, like the sun is blaring down on us inside Rosario's Market, but I can't help it. In fact, I can barely breathe as he walks away, a swagger to his hips like he's still coasting by on a skateboard.

Leia sounds exasperated when she says, "Luca's an idiot, but a fun idiot."

My heart might explode from pounding so hard.

"Luca?" I say.

"He works in the deli."

"Does he go to school with us, too?"

Is it possible I missed him, along with Leia?

"No. He goes to Catholic school—Gonzaga Prep." Then Leia corrects herself. "Though I'm not sure how often he actually *goes* to school."

My eyes won't seem to move from the spot where he was. I've seen people with similar auras—matching shades of orange or pink or green.

But no one has ever been Lizzie's color. *No one.*

She is the only one who blazes cadmium yellow. The color of the sun. Or so I thought.

"Luca," I say again.

"Sometimes all it takes is one person to make swimming in a sea of shit better, you know." Leia gestures all around us. "Welcome to my

31

sea of shit, but if I want to go to college out of state, I need this job." She takes me by the arm again. "Come on. I'll show you where the essential oils are."

As we make our way to a new aisle, I can't help but look over my shoulder at the streak of sunshine left on the floor where Luca stood.

In the end I don't have the courage to deviate from the list. My cart is still filled with garbage that might give Chief and me cancer. But change is not that easy.

Still, I grab a bottle of patchouli oil. No one likes to be sad *and* filled to the brim with shit.

7

MONET'S GARDEN

Lizzie started sending me postcards in third grade, when she found me crying because I wasn't invited to Regan Trentini's birthday party and the rest of my class was. Regan had forgotten me, like so many others. Lizzie asked me to paint flowers on her walls that day.

"As many as you want. How about tulips, Songbird? Can you paint me those?"

"But they bloom in the spring, and this is a summer forest."

"Who cares about science? In *our* world tulips bloom in the summer."

And people aren't left behind to wilt. That's what Lizzie was trying to say.

A week later her first postcard dropped through the mail slot in our front door—addressed to Wren Plumley. On the front was a picture of the Empire State Building.

Dear Wren,

People look like ants from up here, and you know what they say about ants—they can carry two hundred times their weight. Maybe we're really ants in the universe, which means we can carry a lot of baggage and still survive. I know life feels like a lot sometimes, but you can handle it.

I love you,

Mom

Wren Plumley
20080 21st Ave.
Spokane, WA 99203

"See, Songbird," Lizzie said. "She's thinking about you. You're not forgotten. A person doesn't need to be present to be remembered." But I could tell from the look on her face and the wink she gave me that Lizzie had actually sent the postcard.

And it was perfect.

After that a new one came every few months. Some would apologize for missing school performances, some would ask whether I was getting good grades and cleaning my room, some even hinted at a future when we would all be together as a family again.

For a while it worked.

For a while it felt real.

But reality has a way of dimming imagination as we age.

It's been over four years since Lizzie sent me a postcard.

After unloading the groceries, with Chief asleep upstairs, I sift through a stack of week-old mail—junk magazines and Valpak and Publishers Clearing House mailers. I get why people keep this junk.

Hope.

Hope that one day you won't be poor because the Publishers Clearing House Prize Patrol will come to your door with balloons and cameras and give you a gigantic check for $1 million, all because you didn't throw out the one thing that most people do.

I know that feeling, but I still toss the Publishers Clearing House mailer into the recycling bin.

And then a card freezes me in place.

A postcard.

Blue Water Lilies, 1916–1919
 	
 Dear Songbird,
     Have you ever noticed that water lilies grow in polluted lakes? More proof that beauty can be found even among life's garbage. Maybe that's why Monet painted this—as a reminder.
     Sometimes beauty breaks through even the murkiest, smelliest, most contaminated lakes, and the next thing you know, a frog will take a rest on a lily pad in the sunshine.
     I love you,
     Lizzie
	Wren Plumley
	 20080 21st Ave.
	 Spokane, WA 99203

Light comes through the window of the kitchen, as if to illuminate the words. It's a sign.

She's back.

I run around the house, postcard in hand, checking each room for Lizzie. Behind the sofa, in her closet, under the kitchen table, until I'm in the backyard searching the bushes and trees and air for any sign of her. But the clouds have covered the sun now, and I'm still holding a postcard from a person who no longer lives here.

The postcard has no return address. It's postmarked from London, a place Lizzie couldn't possibly be, considering she has no passport. I do a quick search on my phone and figure out the postcard was made on a mobile app called PostIt, a company out of England. It's impossible to track where it was created.

I climb to the roof of the garage and sit with my knees in tight, arms wrapped around my body as if to hold myself together, when really, I'm just holding myself in.

"Where are you, Lizzie?" I ask the lilies in Monet's garden, imagining the sound of a frog echoing from somewhere on the water.

8

THE TRUTH ABOUT WET UNDERWEAR

I'm on the roof when Wilder's light comes on again. It's dark outside, and Chief is at work. Olga is watching TV on the couch in the living room, where she'll eventually fall asleep. She's barely said a word to me.

Chief wasn't happy to see me up here again. It's too far off the ground, and he's seen what people are capable of even when they have two solid feet on the earth.

Some days I really wish he wasn't a police officer.

When Wilder comes to the window, I give a slight wave from my perch. A moment later a text comes through to my phone.

Wilder: Wyd up there?

Me: Waiting for the sun to rise

Wilder: It might be a bit

I look down at Lizzie's postcard.

Me: I'm a little worried about that

Wilder: Is that y ur sad?

Yes, I think to myself. But it's more than that. It's . . . me.

Wilder: Do u want some company while u wait?

Me: That would be nice

Wilder: That's me

Wilder: Mr. Nice Guy

I giggle.

Me: Do u want to come sit on the roof with me, Mr. Nice Guy?

Wilder: Unfortunately I can't

Me: Why not?

Wilder: I get sick when I go outside

Me: Are u a vampire or something?

Me: I hear we have a few of those in WA

Wilder: ☺ I'm not cool enough to be a vampire

Me: Same

Wilder: We're the perfect pair then

At that I can't help but grin down at my phone.

Me: If ur not a vampire what is wrong with u?

Wilder: IDK no one can figure it out

Me: So u just stay inside all day?

Me: Doing what?

Wilder: Waiting just like u

Me: For what?

Wilder: My life to show up

He tells me that he's lived almost his entire life indoors. How no doctor has ever been able to diagnose what's wrong with him, but every time he went outside when he was little, he'd get a fever and a cough and a runny nose and be in bed for days. And it was awful, so he just stopped going outside.

Wilder: It wasn't worth the risk

He moved from Seattle to live with his grandparents in Spokane, where the air is drier. They're hoping it might help.

Wilder: So far I'm too afraid to even open my window

Wilder: What if I get sick again? Then no place is safe

Wilder: It just feels easier to stay inside

The silhouette standing in the window almost looks too skinny to be an actual person, almost like he's disappearing into the light.

Wilder: Want me to entertain you?

Me: How?

Wilder: I'm a well of useless information

Me: Like what?

Wilder: Did u know chickens are attracted to beautiful people?

Me: Swear?

Wilder: I read about it in a research paper

Me: What else?

Wilder: Coke was originally green

Me: Gross

Wilder: Exactly

Wilder: No one wants to drink something green

Wilder: Even if it is delicious

Before I can respond, Olga sticks her head out of the back door. Her poorly maintained blond hair sharply contrasts her black eyebrows, and she's wearing too much makeup for a person whose job it is to sleep. She's clearly annoyed when she finds me on the roof.

"I'm going to bed," she says in a thick Russian accent. When I don't budge, she groans. "Don't make my job any harder than it already is. Come down from that roof, Wren. Your dad don't like you up there."

The silhouette in the attic window is gone, as if Wilder is hiding, but the light remains on.

"I'll come inside in a minute."

Olga closes the door with too much vigor.

My phone rings with a text.

Wilder: Ur name is Wren?

He's back, standing in the window. Even though I can't see his eyes clearly, it feels like we're looking at each other, like we're connected somehow.

Me: Yes

Wilder: Do u ever think about flying away?

I'm too scared, I think to myself, unable to muster the courage to type it. When I don't type anything back, Wilder texts again.

Wilder: Someone did research to find out if wet underwear is uncomfortable

Me: That seems pretty obvious

Wilder: Apparently even the obvious needs to be researched

Me: The findings?

Wilder: Wet underwear is uncomfortable

Me: Mind blown

"Wren!" Olga's voice bellows from inside the house. "Get your butt down from that roof! I need sleep!"

Me: Gimme a sec

I climb down from the roof and bypass Olga on the couch, then go straight to my room and turn on the light. At the window across from mine, Wilder stands, phone in hand, waiting for me. I can see him clearly now, his hair and eyes, his too-thin body. The space around him, that lack of an aura. I know it's wrong to feel comfort in that, but we're the same. No one has ever been like me. For the first time, I don't feel so lonely.

He smiles, and I swear that the stars just starting to appear in the sky get brighter.

Me: Ever noticed that birds only need a bit of light to sing in the morning?

Me: Just a sliver and the chorus starts

Wilder: If that's the case I hope the sun comes out tmrw

I press my nose to the glass, my breath fogging the window.
Wilder does the same.
"Good night," I say, my words trapped inside my room.
Good night, he mouths back.
The light in his room goes out a moment later.

9

CADMIUM YELLOW

Safer on Wheels Driving School is located in an old strip mall, probably filled with asbestos, south of town. The ceiling tile has water damage, and the fluorescent lights cast a gloomy, unhealthy glow on everyone who walks in. Outside the sun shines. I lean my head back against the chair and stare up at the lights until my vision starts to pepper with black spots. The seat next to me remains empty, along with the rest of the row, and I'd like it to stay that way.

It's a Washington State requirement that all teenagers looking to acquire a license must attend thirty hours of classroom instruction in person. The irony of having to attend driving school is that I had to take the bus to get here, since Chief is working the graveyard shift all week and sleeping by day. But if this is what he needs in order to believe I'm "getting back out there," so be it. He hasn't mentioned Utah again, so I won't complain.

Every morning we play *Wheel of Fortune*, eyes forced on puzzles we *can* solve instead of the mysteries that plague our house. It's better that way. If we pretend hard enough that life is fine, eventually it will feel like that—I learned that from Lizzie.

"Take your seats," the overweight, angry-looking teacher states in a monotone voice. Wrinkles around his eyes carve deep ravines in his cheeks, and I can tell that this man is not happy to be here either.

There's a bit of a scramble as people move around, during which someone sneaks in the back of the room and takes a seat in my row at the last second. I glance quickly in his direction and am instantly blinded by cadmium yellow. It blazes so brightly, I have to close my eyes.

Again?

"Shit," I whisper to myself.

When I peek to check if I'm actually seeing the color correctly, Luca, the boy from the grocery store, is at the end of the row, staring at me.

My heart rate surges again, and my head swims. *I will not pass out,* I repeat to myself. *I will not pass out.*

Nothing about Luca's appearance screams yellow. In fact, he's dressed head to toe in black—a tight black shirt, black jeans with rips in the knees. The nose ring dangling from the center of his nose . . . is black. Even his hair is black. But his eyes are another story. They're cinnamon brown. None of this outdoes the cadmium yellow.

He's blinding.

He's overwhelming.

He's staring at me.

I move over a few seats, but it doesn't help. In a room filled with dreariness, he is light. Unavoidable and bright and burning, even in this overly air-conditioned room.

I need a distraction, so I start to write Lizzie a letter in my notebook.

Dear Lizzie,

Monet wasn't appreciated by the French until the Americans found interest in his work. Is this how it goes in life? The people closest to you are the least appreciative until some outsider tries to take you away?

My pen taps on the paper. The letter isn't working. I have nowhere to send it anyway. And cadmium yellow seeps into my peripheral view, staining the edges of the paper in light that can't be erased.

I take another quick glance at Luca. He's still looking at me.

Oh no.

With a quick glance at the window, I check for an escape route. I need to hang a piece of my body outside, like Lizzie did in the cruiser. It took me a while to understand why she rolled down the window, her body never fully contained by the car, even when it was freezing outside. She felt trapped. Frostbite means little when you can touch freedom.

But it's sealed shut. The windows at Driver's Ed are strictly to let light in. Nothing can get out. I scribble more to Lizzie.

Remember how you said that if I ever feel overwhelmed, all I have to do is open a window and fly? What do I do if the window is sealed shut?

Frustrated, I rip the letter from my notebook and ball it up. It's useless. I can't even send Lizzie a text. Her phone is shut off or dead or floating in the Spokane River. She never responds, no matter how many texts I send.

And then Luca plops himself in the desk next to me, shoving his skateboard under the seat. Another blinding streak of cadmium yellow hits me.

He needs to turn down his light, but I know from Lizzie that it's impossible.

"I know you," he says.

"No, you don't."

"Yes, I do. I saved your life yesterday."

"No, you didn't. You're the one who knocked me over."

"But I grabbed you before you fell," Luca says. "So I think that negates the crime."

"That's not how it works."

"Says who?"

"The police."

He stares at me for seconds that pile onto seconds and create a mountain of pressure on my chest. I scoot over, needing space.

He scoots closer. "Is something wrong?"

"No." I can't look at him.

"Do I smell or something?"

"What?" I chance a glance at him and catch a scent of the outside. He even smells like sunshine.

"I blame Leia. She's making me wear natural deodorant. According to her, there are all these toxins in real deodorant that cause cancer, but I'm thinking maybe the natural stuff isn't working, because you clearly don't want me close to you." Luca smells his armpit and shrugs. "Smells OK to me, but people never think they stink. It's always someone else. Which is poetically sad, because we all think like that, and we all kind of stink."

He has a point, but I refrain from responding.

"Leia's a totally weird hipster. Probably belongs in Seattle, but you can't change where you're born, right? But seriously, what's worse: Cancer, or a life with chronic BO? Be honest."

"Definitely cancer," I say, and then bite my cheek for responding.

It's not Luca's light that scares me. It's what happens when it goes dark. When a person gets used to bright light, the eyes adjust, the skin warms, every color is accentuated. A person sees the world differently. But when it disappears . . .

It's the fading light I'm afraid of. I can't handle any more darkness.

"Yeah . . . cancer sucks. You're right." He nods. "I guess I'll stick with the natural deodorant. Thanks for your input. I'm Luca, by the way."

"I know who you are."

"You do?" His posture becomes inflated. "What did Leia tell you?"

That he makes working in a sea of shit better. Is Luca the lily pad Lizzie was talking about? But I can't bring myself to say any of that.

He waits, but I stay quiet, so he says, "Seems unfair that you know me, but I don't know you."

"I don't know you."

"You just said you did."

"I said I know who you are. There's a difference."

"I'm intrigued," Luca says. "Explain it to me."

But I see the trick. He just wants me to talk.

When I don't expound, he says, "At least tell me your name. If you don't, I'll just ask Leia."

"Wren."

"As in the bird? Very cool. Do you sing?"

"No."

That's kind of a lie. I know one song.

"Thank God. That would be super weird if you were named after a songbird and you could sing."

Kind of like a boy being named after the Latin word for "light" and having an aura that's freaking yellow and blinding?

I try to take notes on what Mr. Angry Driver's Ed Teacher is saying. Luca leans in, startling me, and whispers in my ear. He definitely doesn't smell bad. His scent is warm and inviting.

"You know you can google all this information." He taps the notebook.

I don't look at him when I respond. "I retain it better this way."

"OK. But don't get too attached to your mind. Eventually we all lose it." He settles back in his seat, arm resting behind his head, legs stretched long. "I'm strictly here for the go-carts."

"Go-carts?" I ask.

"Yeah, we practice driving in go-carts. Didn't you read the brochure?"

No. Chief signed me up. I just went along with it.

47

Luca digs into his backpack and reveals a gigantic sandwich.

He unwraps the roast-beef sandwich and offers me half. "You want some?"

"It's ten in the morning."

"The perfect time for a snack."

"That's a snack?"

"Teenage boys need twenty-five hundred calories a day. I'm just trying to keep up," he says before taking a large bite. After he swallows, he says, "I pilfer sandwiches from Rosario's. But technically I don't consider it *stealing* . . . more like taste testing. I need to know what I'm selling."

He takes another large bite. The sandwich is half-gone already.

"I'd steal one for you," he says in a whispered tone that sends a rush down my spine.

"Why?" The word falls out of my mouth. "You don't even know me."

"We've established that," Luca says. "Sometimes you don't need to know. Sometimes a person can just tell."

"Tell what?"

"You're worth it."

Sweat trickles down my back, cool. My nerves are practically shot.

"Don't steal for me," I say, squaring myself to the front of the room. "Leia will kill you if you get fired."

"OK," he says nonchalantly, creating space between us again. He puts his head down on the desk, eyes gazing lazily in my direction as another wave of yellow hits me. "I'm entering a food coma, Wren. I'm not going to make it. Fill me in later?"

Luca sleeps through the entire two-hour lesson on Washington State driving laws. I stare out the window, half listening, eyes on the passing cars and the heat that radiates from the asphalt and distorts the air with warmth.

"Even the air knows how to dance, Songbird," Lizzie said once. "Let it show you how. Follow the breeze." She was twirling around in our front yard, arms out wide, fingers tangling with nothing, her long hair a sprinkler of brown all around her. "Don't be afraid to get dizzy. Sometimes it's better to see life a little blurry. We can easily change the way the world looks if we just start to spin."

But I worried about the moment she'd fall. The moment her foot caught on a tree root. It felt . . . inevitable. And I wanted to be there to catch her.

Lizzie could blur the world because I was there to catch her.

But me . . . I'd just fall.

I knew I could never be like her, like a leaf caught in the wind with no care as to what direction it danced or where it landed.

A few times Mr. Angry Driver's Ed Teacher looks directly at Luca's sleeping frame but doesn't move to wake him up.

When everyone shuffles to leave for the day, Luca finally stirs. He zips up his backpack, grabs his skateboard, and says, "So let's just say you weren't opposed to me stealing for you. What kind of sandwich would you want?"

I don't know how to answer him. Silence is my only defense. It's how Chief and I have survived these past weeks. Maybe even the past sixteen years.

I refuse to feel again the same ache that plagued me the morning I woke up and found Lizzie gone.

It's been over a month, and I'm almost used to living in the ravine Chief and I dug for ourselves. To crawl out now means risking the fall back to reality.

Everyone will eventually leave me.

I saw it on Lizzie's face when I went inside and left her alone to tangle with the wind in the front yard.

I saw it on Chloe's face when she started dating Jay.

I even see it in the crinkle around Chief's eyes, in the way his hands rest on his hips, in the gray-peppered mustache that covers his smile.

Disappointment and regret hold hands as they walk away, and neither looks back.

"A woman who doesn't give up her secrets easily . . . ," Luca says. "Just how I like it."

Through the window, I watch him coast down the street on his skateboard and move through the waves of heat emanating from the pavement, a trail of yellow following him. Luca turns from side to side smoothly, as if one with the wind, as if dancing through the breeze, as if held softly and gently by the atmosphere itself, so that he won't fall, no matter how dizzy he gets. Just like Lizzie did.

His unabashed freedom only makes me want to hold steady that much stronger.

10

SOMEWHERE BETWEEN
TRUDEAU AND ZYWIEC

The fifth floor of the Spokane Public Library is stuffed with secrets. I've decided I need to find one. I'm searching frantically row by row, book by book. It may be the only way to stop the crushing feeling in my chest.

"Why do you come up here, Songbird?" Lizzie asked once, her nose crinkled at the musty smell of books.

"I don't know," I said, running my hand along their spines. "To remind these books they're not forgotten, I guess. Everything deserves a little attention."

I showed Lizzie a paper about whether woodpeckers got headaches.

"Isn't that interesting?" I said. "Doesn't it deserve to be noticed by someone?"

But Lizzie wasn't intrigued by research. To her it wasn't important if a woodpecker got a headache.

"What if the research found out woodpeckers *did* get headaches? What would people do then?" Lizzie asked.

"I don't know."

"That's the problem, Songbird. Depending on what you find in your search, you might be in more trouble than you thought. Before you know it, you're trying to give ibuprofen to all the woodpeckers. Better to just let the woodpecker be . . . a woodpecker. It's not our job to know what's going on in its brain."

In the strangest way, Lizzie made complete sense.

"I have an idea," Lizzie said, taking an old dusty book from the shelf. She told me about this guy in Seattle who stands outside a grocery store, handing everyone who walks past a piece of paper and an envelope. He asks them to write down a secret anonymously and send it to him. When people do, he takes the secrets and hangs them up on display outside the grocery store, so anyone who walks past can read them.

"Why would he do that?" I asked her. "That defeats the purpose of keeping a secret."

"Because he knew secrets weigh you down," Lizzie said. "He was trying to help free people."

"But the secrets are anonymous."

"That's not the point, Songbird. People don't share secrets to help others. They share secrets to unburden themselves. He wanted a place people could unpack their secrets and let them go."

That's when she said we should write down our secrets and hide them in the books in the stacks.

"Anytime we need to unburden ourselves, we know where to come," she said. The only time I'd ever see Lizzie touch a book with affection was when it held a piece of her. All Lizzie ever wanted was to be cared for and held.

These books are secret keepers. Somewhere on the fifth floor of the library, tucked in unknown books, are Lizzie's secrets. And I desperately need to find one.

Maybe then I'll know why she left.

I keep searching, but so far I haven't had any luck. The stacks are enormous, and a few years ago the library reorganized each section. Not that Lizzie would have made it easy. She wouldn't let me see where she hid her secrets, in what book, and I'm sure she wouldn't have put the book back in the right place anyway.

"Promise you won't go looking unless it feels absolutely necessary," she said. "Always remember, Songbird: you might not like what you find."

Right now that threat feels small compared to my desperate need for proof that she was real. Is real.

But for all my searching today, it seems Lizzie's secrets might be lost in the stacks indefinitely.

The sun starts to descend in the sky, and every book I open is empty. Lizzie isn't tucked in their pages. Exhausted, I lean back on the bookshelves and wipe the last tear from my face. My face is swollen. My eyes are red. The tip of my drippy nose aches from wiping it. I won't let Chief see me cry. It will only make things worse.

Then I pick up a piece of paper and write down a secret. I can't stop thinking about Luca. Taking an old *Encyclopaedia Britannica*, volume 12, from the shelf and hiding what I've written somewhere between Trudeau and Zywiec, I let my secret go. For now.

After all, Lizzie wasn't the only one hiding things among the pages.

11

FOR THE LOVE OF CATS

"Baby Girl" McCarty operates the Looff Carousel at Riverfront Park in Spokane. All summer long. She's had the job since she was fourteen, back when she was a vegan who protested on the weekends outside Macy's downtown, with a bucket of red paint to splatter on anyone wearing a leather jacket. That phase lasted only until Chief threatened to arrest her should she decide to ruin anyone else's innocent Saturday.

"We lack tourists to begin with, Katherine," Chief said. "You're scaring the precious few who *do* come to Spokane."

Aside from her mom, Chief is the only person who's ever called her Katherine. To everyone else, it's Baby Girl.

"Please do not stand or leave your chosen location for the duration of your ride. Wait for the carousel to come to a complete stop before exiting." She speaks into a microphone. "As Rūmī said, 'What's wrong with waiting? It's the only surefire way to avoid pregnancy and chlamydia. Patience is protection.' Namaste."

Baby Girl decided to try on Buddhism two months ago, though I'm not sure she's actually done any research. I'm pretty sure Rūmī was a Sufi mystic.

Before Buddhism, Baby Girl was a pothead. And before that she was a runner. Baby Girl tries on personalities like clothing. So far nothing has fit for long. She sheds each persona like a snake sheds skin, and starts all over again. Ever since she and Lizzie became best friends in junior high, Baby Girl's aura has never been a consistent color. It's always a shade of purple, but with every personality shift, the aura morphs, the hue lightening with a little more red or darkening with a swirl of navy. Today she's haloed in eggplant.

The carousel spins around and around in front of me, a blur of people and fake decorated horses. When Baby Girl sees me, she leaves her post in the announcer's box. She's dressed in an old bathrobe. Hair that used to be long, practically down to her butt and knotted into light-brown dreadlocks, is gone now. That suited her only during her weed phase, which lasted the longest of any. I was worried Baby Girl thought she found herself in weed, because sometimes disappearing feels like the only way to be. But she eventually got sick of it. Baby Girl buzzed her hair clean off just a month ago, right after Lizzie left.

"You want a ride, Wren? I'll let you go for free."

"No, thanks. I get nauseous." That's not why I'm here. Just watching the carousel spin makes me queasy.

"The Buddha once said, 'The ride is unavoidable. Don't fight it, and get used to the stomachache.'"

"He really said that?"

"Something like that."

"How's the Buddhism going?" I ask.

"Going. Staying. Heaven. Earth. It's all the same." Baby Girl wipes her shaved head. "The bathrobe is comfortable."

"I didn't know Buddhists wear bathrobes."

"They wear regular robes. This is the best I've got. 'Sometimes you've just got to improvise life.' Jim Carrey said that."

Baby Girl has never been the most accurate person. It's only natural when you don't know who you want to be. "I'm not very good at improvising," I say.

"Practice, Wren. 'Practice makes for more practice, and then you die.' Patanjali said that."

"Patanjali doesn't sound very nice."

"Wise and nice don't always go together."

"I guess that's true," I say.

I was jealous when Lizzie and Baby Girl first became friends, though I should have seen it coming. When Lizzie was little, she collected stray cats. It didn't matter how mangy, ugly, or tattered they were. Whether they were street cats with cuts on their noses or lost house cats with groomed fur, if she found one, she wanted it. Even if it belonged to someone else. Even if it was covered in fleas.

She would hold each cat like a precious soul that needed tending, feed them and give them milk and make cat beds out of blankets and pillows in her room. I'm not sure who followed whom, but Lizzie and each cat were inseparable from the moment she welcomed one home. They were soul mates from the start.

Chief never allowed her to keep them. He's allergic to cats and also thinks they're inherently mean.

"I'm just not a cat person," he said.

"What kind of a person are you?" I asked.

"I'm a person . . . person, I guess. If people took as much care of humans as they take of lost animals, the world would be a better place." Chief glanced at Lizzie, who was snuggling whatever cat had wandered into our lives at that moment. "It's easy to take care of something that doesn't talk back, Wren. Animals are unconditionally loyal. People are selfish. That's the challenge."

I got it then, because at that exact moment, I was envious of the cat Lizzie was holding. I didn't want her to have it either. She held *me* like that sometimes, and I didn't want competition.

Lizzie would sob every time she had to let go of a cat. She would beg and plead, but Chief never bent. After the heartbreak of letting so many cats go, Lizzie got smarter about her choices. If Chief was a people person, Lizzie was sure there were a few stray people she could pick up without Chief turning her down.

Baby Girl started coming to our house every day after school in seventh grade. Lizzie would feed her and brush her hair and dress her in different clothes. She even set up a bed for Baby Girl in her bedroom. The forest on Lizzie's walls was thick with new trees and flowers and butterflies, but she still owned a proper bed. The hammock that now hangs from the ceiling didn't come until later. Lizzie begged Chief for one for years.

"Beds have edges to fall off of, Songbird, but a hammock never lets you down," she said.

Baby Girl and Lizzie would lie there and gaze at the forest sprouting on the walls.

For months it seemed like Baby Girl was constantly at our house, taking up space in Lizzie's universe.

"Why do people call you Baby Girl?" I asked her one time.

"Because that's my name."

"I thought your name was Katherine?"

"That's just what my mom calls me."

According to Lizzie, Baby Girl's parents couldn't agree on a name for her after she was born, and like so many couples do, they called her Baby Girl. The nurse even put it on her birth certificate, expecting that her parents would change the name once they agreed on something.

Apparently Baby Girl's parents never really got along, and her dad never liked any of the names his wife suggested. He refused to call her anything else. Eventually her mom just started calling her Katherine because she liked the name, but her dad never did.

"Why doesn't she go by Katherine?" I asked Lizzie once.

"Because the moment we give a name to something, it suddenly carries the burden of meaning, Songbird. Sometimes it's easier just not to have one."

When Lizzie used my nickname, I knew what she meant. Everyone expects a wren to fly, but I was born with broken, rusted wings.

"What's Baby Girl's burden?" I asked.

Lizzie wouldn't tell me, but soon I discovered Baby Girl's secret on my own. Admittedly I was jealous of how much time Lizzie and Baby Girl spent together, but when I told Chief about the bruises I saw on Baby Girl's body, I swear it was well intended.

I watched from the small crack in the door as Baby Girl changed out of her clothes and into one of Lizzie's shirts. Baby Girl showed Lizzie this bruise on her back that was so mulberry purple and indigo, it looked fake, and then one on her thigh and another on her arm. Lizzie examined Baby Girl's body like it was the most interesting painting she'd ever seen. She caressed Baby Girl's skin as delicately as I'd seen her pet a cat with scratches on its nose. She tended to Baby Girl with love.

Lizzie wasn't disgusted by the bruises. She was mesmerized.

"Isn't it amazing that our bodies contain a rainbow," Lizzie said to Baby Girl. "All someone has to do is push on us a little too hard and we turn colorful." Lizzie caressed a particularly yellowish-green bruise. Then she gestured to the trees on the walls. "You're the rainbow in my forest, Baby Girl. You make everything more beautiful."

But even Lizzie knew rainbows didn't glow in the night sky. They don't belong there. And I knew those bruises didn't come from falling off a bike. They came from fists. I was sick to my stomach.

A day later Chief went to Baby Girl's house with some of his police officer buddies. They were in full uniform, with guns and tasers and badges that sparkled in any light.

And a week after that, Baby Girl's dad moved to Coeur d'Alene, and now she sees him only once a month.

When Lizzie found out what Chief had done, she gave him the silent treatment for over a month. But before she went quiet, Lizzie screamed at Chief like she was using up a lifetime of words. She told him he had no right to go over there.

"I had every right," Chief said. "It's my job to protect people. I'm a mandatory reporter, Lizzie. If I didn't take action, I could lose my job."

"So it was all about you! You don't care about Baby Girl at all!"

"That's not what I mean, and you know it."

But Lizzie didn't see it like that. Her eyes were wild. She radiated love for Baby Girl all over our house that day. It was like a cadmium sun took up residency in our living room, and Lizzie wouldn't stop yelling until the house burned down.

"You think bruises exist only on the outside!" she screamed.

"Child abuse is illegal, Lizzie." Chief always tried to remain calm and logical when Lizzie had fits like this. It started when she was little, with the night terrors. As Lizzie got older, the nightmares no longer discriminated between night and day. Chief thought he could hold her together, but you can't stop the sun. Chief tried to be ice-cold water, but Lizzie hated logic.

"It's my job as a police officer to uphold the law."

Lizzie stormed out of the room and slammed her bedroom door. I followed her, because Chief made everything cold.

I wanted to apologize, but she looked at me with this sadness in her eyes like I'd never seen. Sadness is its own living being. It breathes into a person, clings to her skin, changes people right down to the light in their eyes. Lizzie's dimmed so low that night, I was worried a gust of wind would put it out.

"He just doesn't get it, Songbird," she said. "Some love is better than none at all."

I never confessed that I was the one who told Chief about the bruises. But because of me, Baby Girl's dad was gone. Because of me, love went away. Even if it wasn't the right kind of love.

I knew why Lizzie was upset. She knew a rainbow only shined because of rain. And I was pretty sure she would wear a million bruises just to have our mom back.

Lizzie went silent, and the sun went down on our house. It was so cold inside, I thought I might freeze to death if she didn't start talking again.

So I painted more trees and flowers and butterflies on Lizzie's walls to get her speaking again. I covered her room in stars and sky and reminded her that the sun shines in the darkness, even when we can't see it.

Lately I've been reminding myself of this a lot.

Baby Girl finally says, "I know why you're here, and I already told you. I don't know where Lizzie is."

"I know." I can't help my words seeping out like a deflating balloon. Baby Girl might be the only person who loves Lizzie close to as much as I do. And right now I feel like Lizzie is disintegrating. The longer she's gone, the less concrete her life here is.

"Don't waste your time on the dandelions, Wren."

"What?"

"People prune dandelions, but they're weeds. It's their nature to grow and spread. What's more insane: Constantly pruning something, hoping to change it, or letting the weed be a weed?"

I understand what Baby Girl is telling me, but I don't like it.

"Take it from Robert Frost," she says. "'No matter what road you pick in the woods, in the end, we all turn to gray fuzz and float away.'"

"That's depressing."

"Yes, it is."

I take the patchouli oil from my pocket and offer it to her. "Someone told me this is good for depression."

Baby Girl doesn't just put on a drop. She shakes the bottle, a puddle of oil collecting in her palm, and then she rubs it all over herself.

"Thanks," she says. "I feel better already."

That's when I realize that Lizzie's stray cat is stray once more.

"I'm sorry," I say, the apology long overdue.

"For what?"

For being jealous of her relationship with Lizzie. For not helping her sooner. For thinking only of myself. For being the reason her dad lives in Coeur d'Alene. He still calls her Baby Girl, too. He still can't acknowledge her by name.

But the carousel ride is slowly coming to an end, and Baby Girl needs to get back to work.

"I'm not going anywhere . . . ," I say, "should you need me."

12

AN ELLIPSIS SPEAKS FRENCH

Luca brings a ham-and-swiss-cheese sandwich on a baguette to our second day at Driver's Ed.

"Bonjour, Wren. *Voudriez-vous une bouchée mon sandwich?*" He leans in close enough that I can feel his breath on my cheek as he whispers, "I just said, 'Would you like a bite of my sandwich?' in French. I googled the translation. Isn't technology amazing? What did people do before the internet?"

"Go to the library."

"Yuck. Libraries."

"I love the library."

"And I love that you love libraries. In fact, your love of libraries makes me want to fall in love with libraries. We should go there together. You could show me around. How about it?"

But Luca's use of the word "love" has me all confused. He uses it too freely.

"What?"

"Let's get out of here and go to the library. We don't need this class." Luca grabs his skateboard from under his seat.

"Yes, we do, if we want to get a license."

"I'm more of a public transportation kind of guy." He holds up his board. "There's room for two on this thing."

"No, there isn't."

Luca leans in again, this time way too close, and whispers, "There's always room if you make it."

My mouth is so dry, it makes swallowing a feat.

"And I have five brothers, which means I'm really good at sharing," Luca says.

"Five?"

"Five. Sandwich? I made it myself."

With Luca near, I have an intimate view of his nose ring, and the worst part is, I think it's wonderful and perfect. And he has a scrape on his elbow, and his fingernails are cut really short, and he's got a cowlick on the left side of his hairline that makes his hair sprout like a fan. And his aura is warm. Better than warm. It feels like home.

I finally muster the driest swallow of my life and scoot back. "No, thank you."

"I believe it's *'Non, merci'* in French." Luca wiggles his eyebrows. "Are you impressed yet?"

"Non," I say mockingly, even though I totally am.

"Touché. I'll figure you out one of these days."

I knew this might happen. I worried about it all morning. But there is no getting out of Driver's Ed without alerting Chief, and then he might start talking about Utah again.

He could tell something was off as we watched *Wheel of Fortune* this morning. All I could think about was Luca.

"If I were a punctuation mark, what would I be?" I asked Chief. Contestant Jorge spun the wheel.

"Dear God, not this again," Chief said. He gulped an extra-long swig of beer. "Why do you *have* to be anything? Why categorize yourself?"

I ignored his question. "You're a period."

"How do you figure?"

"You're a full stop. A complete sentence. That's how you see the world. There are subjects, and there are verbs, and you hold them together in the correct place."

"I guess that sounds about right."

"I think I might be a period, too." But for different reasons. After a period comes a new thought. It marks the end. A place where ideas take a turn and never look back.

"You say that like it's a bad thing," Chief said. "There's nothing wrong with being organized and concrete."

"Until you meet an ellipsis."

Lizzie is an ellipsis. She's a thought that goes on and on and on. She's ideas you want to follow. She is infinite. I think our mom was the same. And judging by the look Chief gave me when I said that, I'm probably right.

The problem with a period loving an ellipsis is that the period always wants to contain infinity. A period is just a piece of the ellipsis's puzzle, but it can never be an ellipsis. And loving an ellipsis means constantly searching for something concrete and never finding it. It means searching in books for a truth that doesn't exist.

Caring for an ellipsis means throwing love into the wind and watching it scatter.

I didn't watch to see if Jorge won the bonus puzzle.

Even how Luca sits today, leaning toward me, unafraid and intimate. Engaged not only with me, but around me. Luca is an ellipsis, too. He coasts on the edge, balancing, catching speed as he moves, like a wave. Just like Lizzie. I can't even muster the courage to do a handstand, propped up against a wall, let alone attempt moving *and* balancing on a skateboard at the same time. The best I'll get is the view from the top of the garage. A life of observation, but not engagement. That's my destiny.

And most people live their entire lives never noticing just how many birds float in the sky above them.

I scoot away from Luca. The more distance between us, the better.

"Oh . . . I get it," he says.

"Get what?"

"You're a vegetarian." Luca examines his ham sandwich.

"No, I'm not."

"Jewish and don't eat pork?"

"No," I say more emphatically.

"I swear I don't have cooties. Or herpes. Or gonorrhea. I've never even had sex. Not that you have to have sex to get herpes. At least that's what they tell us in health class. But they also tell us premarital sex is a sin, so . . ." Then Luca winks. "I'd become a sinner for you."

I might pass out.

"Don't worry. We don't have to raise our kids Catholic."

"*What?*" I say, floored.

"I come from a long line of Catholics. We practically founded Gonzaga University. But I'm not set on it. I'm not even sure I like God. What kind of a guy makes premarital sex a sin? I'll tell you: no guy. Which makes me suspicious about the whole thing. I'm thinking someone made it all up."

Luca has rambled so much, I'm lost in his words, just trying to breathe.

"Are you hungry yet?" Luca asks, once again offering me half his sandwich.

He's staring at my lips, and I realize I'm staring at his. They're really nice, kind of perfectly round, not too big and not too small.

"You don't have to give me anything in return," Luca says, quieter now. "Unless you want to give me a piece of your heart?"

"No, thanks." I've never had a harder time saying two words. "You can have the sandwich."

When he finishes it, Luca lays his head down and commences his nap. The silence is grating. I like when he talks.

At the end of class, Luca grabs his skateboard and slings his backpack over his shoulder. "Au revoir, then, Wren."

Even if I wanted to run after him, Luca would sail smoothly past me until all I could see were the places his yellow light touched along the way. A period, endlessly frozen in place, left to watch as an ellipsis moves on.

At the next class, Luca unveils a hotdog from his backpack. It's wrapped in tinfoil. He's even brought little packets of mustard.

"Have you ever googled what a hotdog is made of?" he asks.

"No."

"Don't. You'll never eat one again."

"Have you?"

"Unfortunately, yes, but my stomach outweighs my logic at times." Luca smells the hotdog. "I just don't care that I'm eating pig anus, as long as it tastes good. That's the problem with teenage boys. No frontal lobe. No logic. For example, it is completely illogical that I should have a crush on you."

And the bit of calm I tried to hold on to dissolves.

"And it's a big one. I'm talking epic proportions. Completely illogical. But I can't stop thinking about you. It's crazy. I know."

No one has ever had a crush on me. You have to see someone to want them.

"Now, if I was logical, I'd back off. If a girl doesn't want to share a simple sandwich, she's not interested. But I'm not logical," Luca says. "I might be damn near delusional. It runs in the family."

Luca takes my phone.

"For example, a logical person wouldn't put his phone number in your phone." He types as I watch, unable to move. "A logical person wouldn't text himself so he now has your number."

Luca shows me the text he's just sent from my phone to his. He hands my phone back to me.

"Only an insane person would do this." He types, and a second later a text comes through on my screen.

Luca: Hey

Hesitantly, I type back.

Me: Hi

Cadmium yellow radiates all around us in beams and streaks, and it feels permanent. When I breathe, I swear I take in not only air but his essence as well.

"Sometimes it's good to be illogical," he says, and then takes a bite of his hotdog. "Keeps life interesting."

My eyes drift down to Luca's nose ring and then to the smirk on his face and to his ratty T-shirt and then back up to his eyes, which might be cradling me.

"Aren't you going to ask if I want half of your hot dog?"

"No. It's time you meet me *half*way. Get it?" Luca's grin is goofy and cute, a smile to turn a person inside out. He finishes the hotdog and lays his head down on the desk.

"When you're ready, Wren, you have my number."

13

I'M CURSED

I sit in my window, waiting, needing Wilder's light to come on. The noise of the reality-television show Olga is watching echoes up the stairs, making its way through our vacant house as if to point out all the empty places.

Chief is working tonight. Luca's text is pulled up on my phone. I can't stop staring at it.

How did this happen? How did *I* let this happen? I know better, and I need to fix it, and yet I don't know how. Or . . . maybe . . .

If I'm honest . . .

I'm not sure I want to.

My fingers tingle with warmth, itching to text him again. The memory of his whisper on my cheek lingers in my pores, sweet. How did Luca suddenly become a concrete person in my life?

I rub my cheek clean and shake out my hands, the uncomfortable itch of anxiety nestled in my stomach. It's coming. To *be* really means to be known. Seen. Acknowledged. But nothing lasts. Eventually someone leaves.

I felt it the night before Lizzie crept out of the house—the uneasy ache right before someone leaves. Part of me knew it was coming. The leaving is so much a part of me, it's as constant as breathing—the in and the inevitable out.

People make choices before they take action. For some it's coded in their DNA. It's in the makeup of their bones and hair and eyes. The gleam of wanting more shimmered in everything Lizzie did. Anyone who met her couldn't help but be instantly drawn in.

Like a cold front that comes down over the mountains and settles in the valley of Spokane, I felt it creep closer and closer. And yet every morning when Lizzie was in her hammock, swaying to an artificial breeze, I was relieved. I convinced myself I was being paranoid. It wasn't time yet. She wouldn't do this to me.

But hope is fickle. And when it leaves, fear takes its place.

Lizzie didn't leave a note. She didn't kiss me goodbye. She didn't hold my hand. She just let go. She snuck out when neither Chief nor I could grab her, when not even the law that Chief follows, day by day, night by night, could bring her home. All she left were the clothes in the closet and an empty hammock.

It's not her fault, though.

I am made of discarded love, and anyone who holds me feels its use, its wear, feels the holes and the tears and the snags. Even Lizzie, who shopped for clothes at thrift stores because she felt bad for castaway T-shirts and old, worn-out belts desperate to hold someone again. At some point secondhand T-shirts become unwearable and turn to rags.

The light next door comes on. When Wilder sees me standing there, a text rings through immediately.

Wilder: Wanna know what I learned today?

Me: What?

Wilder: Bacon can cure nosebleeds

Wilder: As if we needed another reason to eat bacon

The anxiety resting on my chest eases somewhat.

Wilder: Now u tell me something

Me: I read once that if u name a cow it produces more milk

Wilder: Fascinating

Wilder: Tell me something else

I tell Wilder that the oldest bird's nest ever found on earth is twenty-five hundred years old and that in Mexico birds use cigarette butts to make their nests.

Me: They make a home from discarded items

Me: A feather

Me: A twig

Me: A string

Wilder: Don't forget the cigarette butts

Anytime Lizzie came into my room, she'd look at the blank white walls and neatly made bed and properly folded laundry and she'd say, "You can't build a nest here, Songbird. Come into my room, and take one of my trees. They belong to you anyway."

As if it were that easy. As if I could peel a tree from her wall and put it on mine. I wouldn't do that to Lizzie, because I knew she'd miss that tree. She'd long to swing on its branches and feel the wind in her hair. If a tree went missing, a vacant space would live in Lizzie's heart, and she'd leave me even sooner. But I can handle the space.

I left the trees just where they were, because Lizzie's love was more important than collecting pieces to build a home. *She* was my home.

I stand to face Wilder in the window. His hand presses to the glass, as if he wishes he could push through it and let fresh air in.

Wilder: What's wrong?

Me: I'm cursed

I was made by two people clawing at the bottom of life for more only to find dead twigs and dried leaves and loose string and cigarette butts, and for just a while they made a nest. But time destroys homes that flimsy.

Me: Everyone ends up leaving me behind

I shouldn't be happy that Wilder is sick. That he's locked up in a house, unable to leave. But for once in my life, I don't feel so alone.

Wilder: I'm not going anywhere

Me: So it's u and me?

Wilder: Together

Haystacks on a Foggy Morning, 1891

Dear Songbird,
Monet painted haystacks twenty-five times to capture what they look like in different light. He knew that nothing is the same day after day. We all change, even though we think we're the same. The haystacks are proof.
Let the light change the picture. You might see a different you.
I love you,
Lizzie

Wren Plumley
20080 21st Ave.
Spokane, WA 99203

14

BLURRED LINES

It's Sunday. The wagon is in front of Rosario's Market. Chief's list is in my hands. The mechanical horse sits unridden, baking in the sunlight. I'm not sure how many pennies are in the jar hidden in my closet, but I have to imagine it's enough to buy something. Maybe even freedom. The horse is watching me. Waiting.

Today Leia teaches me about reading food labels. And I want to learn, but it's hard to concentrate knowing Luca might be somewhere in the store. My heart's not really in it. It keeps wandering the aisles, trying to get a peek at Luca and his nose ring.

"You know what the food industry wants you to do?" Leia asks me.

"What?"

"Stay naïve. They don't want you to read labels. They want you sitting on a couch, playing video games and stuffing your mouth with Doritos. But they don't want you to know what's in Doritos. They just want you to *want* them. Kind of like boys. But the truth is, when you get up close, boys smell really bad."

I haven't been up close with many boys, or any at all until recently, but that has not been my experience. Luca smells like sunshine and possibility.

I keep finding his scent lingering on my clothes. Or maybe I'm imagining it, but just because something is imagined doesn't mean it isn't real.

"What's in Doritos?" I ask, focusing on Leia.

"MSG, among other things."

Leia is so alive when she talks about carcinogens and the "bullshit legal system that protects food companies all in the name of 'flavor secrets' when the majority of Americans are consuming poison and dying of obesity, clogged arteries, and cancer." I can't help but be in awe.

"We can't survive without food," she says. "It might be the longest relationship we'll ever have, and yet we let it treat us like shit. What if food was a friend? Do you want a friend who's nice on the outside and tastes great in the moment but afterward you're riddled with a stomach-ache and regret from binge eating an entire carton of hormone-injected ice cream? Or do you want a friend who has nothing to hide? What you see is what you get."

A visual of Chloe meanders through my mind. She hasn't texted me, and she wasn't at the weekly softball game last night. I was thankful for that. Her mom said she was out with Jay.

"You know me, I'm not one to tout my own kids," she said, "but by God that Chloe has found herself one cute boyfriend. And he's sweet. You should see how he dotes on her."

"May God have mercy on her soul," I said, as Anne Boleyn's head rolled in the grass. Proverbially speaking. I wanted to gag. Jay is geneti-cally modified food—bulky, tastes good, looks even better, but is high-school poison.

Today Leia is wearing a new pin. This one says, **I TALK TRASH.**

"What does that one mean?" I ask.

"It's one of my things—composting and recycling. Did you know there's a plastic island made from the shit people didn't care to recycle, floating in the middle of the Pacific Ocean? And it's a tourist attraction! If that isn't representative of how messed up this world is, I don't know what is. Thank God for patchouli oil."

Leia dabs some on her wrist before offering me the bottle.

I know some things make her sad, but she's so alive that I want to reach out and grab her turquoise-blue aura like it's something tangible. Like maybe I could swim in it, letting it seep into my pores. Sadness and all.

"What are some of your other things?" I ask.

"Overalls." She gestures to her outfit. "Glitter, but it's terrible for the environment, so I don't use it often. And Roller Derby."

"What?"

"You're looking at Princess Lay-Her-Out."

"What does that mean?"

"I'm a roller girl," she continues, "a jammer for the Crazy Daisies Roller Derby team. It's a junior league."

"What's a jammer?"

"It's basically my job to kick some ass and not get knocked over in the process."

"Sounds . . . crazy."

"It's awesome," Leia says. "There's nothing like knocking over a bunch of badass chicks to release some emotion. What about you? What's your *thing*?"

"I don't really have a thing."

"Everyone has a thing," she says.

Lizzie was my every*thing*. But now . . .

I could tell her about how I see auras. How the turquoise blue that surrounds Leia only makes her more beautiful. How when I look at a painting by Monet, I want to cry because it's so brilliant. How he understood the human condition—that the moment we put concrete lines on a canvas, we've taken the imagination away. The possibility for more, for interpretation. That life is distorted and blurred and should be represented as such.

I could also tell her how I used to paint, how there was so much more I wanted to put on Lizzie's walls and in our universe, but since she left, I can't seem to do it. Some mornings I wake up desperate to hold a brush in my hand. To create something from nothing.

"Does it really feel that good to knock people over?" I ask, a lump stuffed deep in my throat.

"Yes."

"Aren't you worried they might knock you over, too?"

"Sure, but that's what makes it exciting."

"I've never knocked anyone over."

"You're young. There's time." And then Leia gets animated and says, "Oh my God. You should join the league!"

I'm too weak for that. Leia is covered in lean muscle, whereas I am simply covered in fragile skin. I don't think I'm strong enough to handle blow after blow right now.

But I don't get to respond, because at that exact moment, Luca turns down the aisle, ever so casually, his cadmium-yellow aura encasing him delightfully. Warmly. He's wearing a red apron, but underneath it a tight blue shirt hugs his frame. He's all primary colors, and I think for just a moment that maybe Luca is the holder of limitless possibilities.

"Leia, I need your help." He's holding a carton of almond milk and regular milk. "Which one should I drink?"

"That all depends," she says sarcastically. "Do you want boobs or not?"

"Depends on whose boobs they are."

Leia groans and takes the cow's milk from Luca's hands. "Drinking this is like taking a shot of estrogen. How do you think they keep cows nursing all the time? Hormones. That's how. And men wonder why they have man-boobs."

"You said it again." Luca grins.

Leia rolls her eyes in my direction. "Men. I told you they stink."

Luca eyes me playfully. "Who's your friend, Princess?"

"This is Wren." Leia gestures in my direction.

"Wren," Luca says. "I believe we've met before."

"Yeah, you knocked her over last week on your skateboard. Dumb ass."

Is that what Luca did? Knocked me over? Is that what this feeling is—the drifting, the light-headedness I feel when he's around, like the ground can't hold me?

"My apologies for the dumb-assery," Luca says. "Can I make it up to you somehow? I make an excellent sandwich."

"No, thanks," I say. "It's not on my list." I flash Chief's tidy grocery list.

"Maybe I can help." He snags it and turns his back on me, reading it like it's a diary or something.

"Actually, I'm not hungry right now," I say more emphatically. "So I don't really need a sandwich. It doesn't fit into my life at the moment . . . I'm full."

That might be the worst lie I've ever told.

Luca turns back around and says, "That's OK. I can be patient. You'll get hungry at some point. And then I'll be here with open arms. Ready to make you a sandwich."

He hands the list back to me. Leia eyes us suspiciously.

"What's going on?" she says to Luca and me.

"Nothing," I say quickly.

And simultaneously Luca says, "Something."

For a moment no one moves. Awkwardness settles around us.

Leia says, "You better watch out, Luca. Wren's going to join the Crazy Daisies. And if you mess with one of us, you mess with us all."

"Really? I love a girl in roller skates."

"I didn't say that." Embarrassed, I look at my feet. "I mean . . . I don't even know how to roller-skate."

"You'll pick it up quickly," Leia says casually. She has no idea how weak I am. How loosely I'm held together. One push . . .

And then Luca says, in a warm tone that trickles down my spine, "I promise, Wren, I won't mess with you."

I'm encased in his light once again, and it feels good. Better than good. It feels like I might actually heal.

But moments never last.

"You better get back to work," Leia says to him.

"Fine. But first tell me again how almonds produce milk," Luca says. "I've never seen a nipple on an almond."

"You're hopeless," Leia says.

"You can't be a failure unless you try." Luca turns and meanders up the aisle. "I guess I'll just have to stick to drinking Gatorade."

"Gatorade?" Leia shouts exasperatedly.

Luca's soft laughter lingers even when his body is gone from sight, but it's as if the air-conditioning has gotten colder. I shiver without him near. And that scares me.

Some days I wish I made drawings with chalk. Then it wouldn't hurt so badly when the picture disappeared after a rainstorm. But oil paint on a canvas . . . The artist knows how many mistakes are painted underneath the masterpiece. Oil can't be erased.

"Doesn't it ever get to you?" I ask Leia. "To care so much, and yet people keep throwing out plastic. People eat food that's poison. People don't change."

"If there's one thing being a roller girl has taught me, it's that pain is a necessary side effect of progress."

I look at Chief's grocery list. Luca added his name to the bottom of it, as if he's an item I'm meant to pick up and take home along with all the other food—another item that will either keep me alive . . . or be the death of me. And Leia has taught me that I need to choose wisely.

Me: Do u miss going outside?

Wilder: Sometimes

It's late, the darkest part of night, when the sun is so gone it's hard to imagine it'll ever come back. And yet if you wait long enough, a dusty gray begins to form on the horizon.

Sometimes I stay up all night just to see it.

Me: What do u miss most?

From my windowsill, I see him, sitting in his room, the light on. Everywhere else in the house is dark, just like mine. We're two lights in a sea of raven black.

Wilder: The smell of grass after it rains

Me: I love that smell

Wilder: Me too

Me: I'd miss the lilacs

Spokane is filled with lilac trees that bloom in May. It's like the entire town is one gigantic flower coming alive after a long, dreary winter. For a while, when the lilacs are out, Spokane seems to forget its struggles. Chief says crime is even lower when Spokane turns into a flower.

Wilder: But there's something I miss even more

Me: What's that?

Wilder: I wish I could hold someone's hand but I'm afraid to touch anyone

At that I face the window full on, my heart aching. Wilder is there, his thin frame taking up such a small portion of the window, his hair vibrant, a sad yet honest smile on his face.

Me: Will u ever get better?

Wilder: IDK

Me: Well until then we can pretend

I place my hand on the window. Wilder mimics me. Our fingers curl at the same time, and I imagine them interlacing, his palm pressing confidently to mine, our hands squeezing closed, sealing us together. Warm skin to warm skin. No fear. It takes the lonely away and heats the cold in the center of me until it's dissolved into nothing. With Wilder I'm on the edge of forgetting.

We stand like this, pretending to touch, until my legs are sore and my eyes are drooping with fatigue. And I think maybe pretending is safer than reality, because when Wilder and I finally turn off our lights, I can still imagine his palm in my hand.

As the gray of morning comes in my window, I finally climb into bed. Before I fall asleep, I send Wilder another text.

Me: Maybe u should open the window

Me: Just to see what might happen

Wilder: I'm not sure it's safe

Me: But if u don't try you'll be locked in there forever

15

DEATH BY HANGMAN

Luca is light, and I am a coward. I don't know how to explain to him that the way he smells like sunshine, the way he casually sits during Driver's Ed, his long legs extending forward, the cadmium yellow that emanates in all directions, warming an overly air-conditioned room, so much so that I want to inch closer and closer to him—it all scares me.

"Good morning, Wren," he says formally, getting a notebook and pen out of his backpack.

"No sandwich today?"

"I'm trying something new this week."

"What's that?"

"I'm going to stay awake." Luca makes the statement proudly. "My grandma told me that no girl wants to date a failure, so . . . I'm changing. Maybe I've been wrong all along. But that changes today. I figure I try pretty damn hard *not* to work. Why not take that effort and put it toward . . . working? So from now on, you're my marshmallow."

"What does that mean?"

"Delayed gratification. I thought success came to those who tried, but it turns out success comes to those who wait."

"What does that have to do with a marshmallow?"

"It was a behavior experiment," Luca says. He opens his empty notebook and writes down the date. "Kids were offered a marshmallow. They could eat it or wait. If a kid decided to wait, they'd get another marshmallow. Turns out, the kids who waited became more successful in life. Hence . . . you're my marshmallow. Though if all of a sudden there were two of you, I don't think I could handle it. It's hard enough sitting next to *one* of you."

My cheeks heat instantly. "You think you can change just like that?"

"I can try . . . or maybe it's more . . . I can wait," Luca says. "The world is changed by people who simply attempt something new. Take Rodney Mullen. What if he never attempted a kickflip? A heelflip? A three-sixty flip? Where would the world be? The man basically created skateboarding as we know it."

When he talks about skateboarding, it's like Luca is speaking a different language.

"You really like skateboarding, don't you?"

Luca becomes effervescent. "Yes!"

"Why?" I ask.

He leans in close. "The rush."

And I can't help but repeat, breathlessly, "The rush?" because he's so close, and I don't care what Leia says—not all boys stink.

"Yeah," Luca says. "The rush—nothing is better."

"Nothing?"

"Well, I suspect kissing you is *way* better, but I have yet to do that." Luca licks his lips, and I realize I'm staring again. An infectious smile pulls Luca's face. "Give me your hand."

"No."

"Please?"

"Why?"

Luca shakes his head. "Just this once, no questions. Just trust me."

I reach out hesitantly. Luca grabs ahold of my hand so strongly, there's no option to pull back. He places it on his chest, directly over his heart.

"I solemnly swear I will not fall asleep in class today."

His chest is warm, the cotton of his T-shirt soft. Something happens to me. A rush. A wave of light-headedness. Of pure goodness. The moment of connection seems so worth it, no matter the consequences.

If this is the rush he's talking about, then I understand why he skateboards all the time. Who worries about a broken arm when something feels this good?

But too soon Luca lets my hand go and squares himself toward the teacher, pencil in hand, and the longing sets in.

I keep glancing at the place on his shirt where my hand was, as if a piece of myself was left there and I can't decide if I want to take it back. That sliver of myself could go missing, lodged in a sidewalk crack or left in a cold, abandoned building.

No more than twenty minutes into the two-hour session, Luca starts shifting in his seat.

"Are you OK?" I whisper.

"Fine. Totally fine. This stuff is fascinating," he says, holding his eyes open. "Who knew you're supposed to stop at a red light? Or use a turn signal? Or wear your seat belt? Consider my mind blown."

Five minutes later he says, "OK, I'm dying, Wren. I need you."

The teacher coughs, signaling for both of us to pay attention.

"For what?" I whisper.

Luca scoots his chair closer to me and starts scribbling in his notebook. He passes it to me, pointing to the question he's written at the top of the page.

Pick a letter?

Underneath he has drawn a hangman.

Of all the games he could have chosen, Luca picks one shockingly similar to *Wheel of Fortune*, making him feel even more familiar.

When I don't give a letter instantly, he becomes more insistent, this pleading, pathetic look on his face. I write down the letter *T*.

The puzzle has two *T*s.

Luca taps the paper impatiently.

"What happened to waiting?" I whisper.

He gestures to the hangman. "This is clearly life or death, Wren."

I write a letter *S*.

He draws a circle for a head on the hangman and smirks.

I write an *E*.

Luca fills in one space with the letter *E*, but the puzzle isn't filled in enough to solve. The letter *R* gets a stick body added to the hangman's head. I grunt, annoyed.

"Now you know how I feel," Luca whispers. "When you want something, but you can't quite get it."

I carry on as if his statement doesn't send me spinning, twirling, thinking, wanting. My hangman is already gaining body parts. I can't let him die. The puzzle is barely filled in.

___ ___ ___ ___ / ___ ___ ___ / ___ ___ / ___ ___ T / ___

___ T ___ / ___ E?

My next choice is *O*. My hangman lives on.

___ ___ ___ ___ / ___ O ___ / ___ O / O ___ T / ___ ___

T ___ / ___ E?

The next two letters are giveaways—*Y* and *U*—and the phrase starts to take more shape.

__ __ __ __ / Y O U / __ O / O U T / __ __ T
__ / __ E?

My next two guesses are *C*, which gains the hangman an arm, and *M*. Another space is filled. The answer is so close I can feel it. My next guess is *L*.

__ __ L L / Y O U / __ O / O U T / __ __ T __ / M E?

The solution comes to me so quickly, I don't have time to think before it tumbles out of my mouth, too loudly to take back.

"Will you go out with me!"

The class goes silent. The kind of silent that actually has a sound, like too much pressure in your ears.

A grin is plastered to Luca's face.

"Well, if you insist," he says.

The entire class looks at us. Mr. Angry Driver's Ed Teacher crosses his arms over his large belly.

"Wait. What?" I say, confused.

"Are you two done with this ridiculous display of teenage hormones?" the teacher asks.

"Yes," Luca says. "Sorry, sir. Proceed. What were you just saying about the gear shift? The *P* stands for 'Park'? Captivating. What an inspiration to teach such riveting material." When the teacher starts up again, Luca whispers, "Sorry. I guess I failed the Marshmallow Test, but whatever, marshmallows are delicious. I don't need two of you. One is perfect."

His posture has shifted. He's rejuvenated.

"My grandma was right about one thing, and that rarely happens these days. Staying awake in Driver's Ed can lead to positive changes in my life."

I'm glad he sees it that way. I, on the other hand, am drowning. It's hard to breathe. I've never been on a date before. I've never even kissed anyone. Not a peck or a smooch or a passing, accidental cheek kiss. What have I done?

When we're dismissed, Luca stands and says, "I'll pick you up at seven. Tomorrow. Wear something comfortable."

"Tomorrow?" I snap.

Gracefully, he slings his backpack on, smooth and easy, like everything else Luca does. I can't move.

"What about all that talk of being patient?" I ask. "Waiting for me to come to you?"

"Leia says we need to be the change we want to see. I want to *be* with you, so I'm making that change happen."

"Why?" The question slips out in a whimper. "You barely know me."

"Why does that matter, Wren? We all start out as strangers. Even love grows from a state of loneliness."

He turns to leave, and I say, "Make it eight." Chief will be at work then, and I won't have to explain myself.

"I guess waiting *one* more hour won't kill me."

As he rides down the street, I see the piece of my heart dangling off his T-shirt and catching the breeze as Luca sails over the concrete beneath his board. I'm hanging on by a thread. One wrong move and the sliver of me Luca carries will be cut free, only to get caught in the air and drift away. And yet I'm not reaching out to take it back.

My choice has been made.

He can have me.

16

MIRROR IMAGE

The carousel ride is just coming to a stop when Baby Girl sees me approach.

"Be mindful exiting the ride," she says into the microphone when the cheerful music-box tune has stopped. "Remember what Gandhi said. 'If we all just stopped stepping on each other's feet, our shoes would last longer.' Have a beautiful day in the great city of Spokane. Namaste."

She's still dressed in her bathrobe, her aura of eggplant purple intact.

"Don't you get sick of this music?" I ask her. "It's the same annoying tune over and over again."

"It's symbolic."

"Of what?"

"Life," she says. "You want a ride?"

"No, thanks." I'm nauseous enough as it is, and time is ticking. Every second brings me closer to tomorrow night, and Luca.

"Have you ever been on a date?"

"What kind of date?"

"There are different kinds?"

"Of course. There's a friendly date, a hookup date, a 'get drunk and have sex' date, a 'get high and watch Netflix date' . . . and then there's a *date*-date."

"How can you tell if it's a date-date?"

"It's a night you'll never forget. That's why you remember the *date*."

"I think I have a date-date tomorrow," I say pathetically. "I don't even know what to wear."

Lizzie should be here. I don't want to be mad at her, because anger never brings anyone home, but I can't seem to stop it.

"Will you help me?" I ask Baby Girl.

"I'm no help. I've never been on that kind of a date." She walks back to the carousel. "Sorry, Wren, the ride must continue."

"Please!" I blurt out. "After all, Martin Luther King Jr. said 'help' is a four-letter word. Imagine what would happen if people spoke of help instead of shit."

"He didn't say that." But she stops. "I can come over after my shift tomorrow. It ends at four."

"Thank you."

Baby Girl starts the carousel for a new set of riders. And the music plays on.

Impression, Sunrise, 1872

Dear Songbird,
Did you know a critic used the word
"impressionist" to ridicule Monet about this
painting? But did Monet change his art? No.
He stayed true to his heart and forced
the world to start seeing through different
eyes.
I love you,
Lizzie

Wren Plumley
20080 21st Ave.
Spokane, WA 99203

My closet is a mess of nothing. I can't wear anything I own. We've been through all of my clothes, and nothing is date-date worthy.

"What about Lizzie's closet?" Baby Girl suggests.

She drags me down the hallway to Lizzie's room. I haven't spent much time there since she left. Without Lizzie there, trees that used to feel real don't so much anymore.

The late-afternoon sun comes through the window, casting a warm glow on the forest and sky. It almost looks like it's daytime in the perpetual night painted on Lizzie's walls.

Baby Girl rummages around Lizzie's closet as I run my hands over the painted trees. We're the only two people in the house right now. Chief is at the gym.

I didn't tell him about my date. Boys are not a part of the routine. Chief would ask questions. He might even call out of work just to meet Luca, and while he wouldn't be in uniform, he's always wearing a gun. And a mustache.

"Let's see what Lizzie left behind," Baby Girl says, throwing clothes on the floor and ordering me to try them on. But I can't seem to. The pile grows and grows, but I know I won't find anything for me among Lizzie's secondhand clothes.

Instead I lie down in the hammock. The room still smells like Lizzie, like sunshine in the twilight. But there's something wrong with the room now, and it's not just that Lizzie isn't here. I can't quite figure out what it is.

"Do you think she's going to come home?" I ask Baby Girl. My question makes her pause, a pair of cutoff shorts and a flowery, flowing shirt in her hands. "Never mind. You don't have to answer that."

Baby Girl sits down on the floor next to me. It's as if we're lost in the woods at night. Even the carpet feels like grass beneath us.

"We never know anything for certain," Baby Girl says.

"Who said that?"

"Me."

"You're wiser than you think."

The starry sky above me feels inaccurate now. I've spent time staring at the stars from my perch on the roof, and looking at the ones I painted, and I wonder if I ever saw stars properly until Lizzie left.

Baby Girl gently rocks me side to side, like the wind does to the trees, like a mother does to a baby. The movement is so habitual, I know she must have done this many times to Lizzie.

"You have two options, Wren," Baby Girl says. She gestures to the woods around us. "Seek or surrender."

"Meaning?"

"Hope you're going to find something out there, or stay scared of what might exist."

"I kind of like you as a Buddhist," I say.

"I don't know . . ." Baby Girl examines her worn-out bathrobe. "I'm not so sure I'm cut out for it. It was comfortable for a while."

"What will you be next?"

"I haven't decided." She holds Lizzie's flowing top up to her own torso.

I don't know if Baby Girl tries on different personas because she doesn't know who she is or because she's afraid to be herself. Her dad pushed and prodded and squashed the person she was, made her think she wasn't good enough, until one day Baby Girl vanished. Ever since, she's been searching for a person to be who's worth loving. And that I understand.

"Take it," I say. "Take all of it."

"Seriously?"

Baby Girl exchanges her bathrobe for Lizzie's top and a pair of cutoffs, shedding an old personality for a new one right before my eyes. She makes it look so easy, but maybe that's why none of them sticks. If being yourself were as comfortable as Buddhism, everyone would do it.

Baby Girl checks herself in the mirror that hangs in the closet. Her aura changes to a different shade of purple. This time it's mauve.

"It fits you perfectly," I say.

With Baby Girl dressed in Lizzie's clothes, here in Lizzie's room, for a brief second our house feels like it used to. Like love just walked in and took a seat on the floor next to me.

What was so wrong with my and Chief's love that Lizzie left? Sure, it wasn't always obvious. Sometimes we had to dig in the couch cushions in search of it, where it hid among the coins and lost hair bands. Maybe sometimes it was dressed in yelling and cursing and crying. But if a person looked closely, felt between the cracks, a sliver of love could be pulled free.

A person doesn't walk away from love unless it hurts too much to stay.

That's how it was with our mom. We were too small to remember her when she left, so instead of missing a mom who chose to leave us, Lizzie and I created a person we needed—a person so extraordinary, our small life couldn't contain her. Her *only* option was to leave.

But a person feels what's missing, even when it's something she can't remember.

And Lizzie? What was her pain? I thought I knew it all because we shared the same story, but I'm starting to think there's more—more she didn't tell me.

"Maybe you could be my sister," I say to Baby Girl. "For your next persona. Just try it on while Lizzie's gone. Since the clothes fit and all."

And after a moment Baby Girl says, "OK. Tell me what Lizzie would do."

So I tell Baby Girl about the game we'd play, imagining all the places our mom could be and all the things she could be doing instead of being with us.

"Like in Doctors Without Borders, somewhere in Uganda," I say.

"Or helping with hurricane relief in Puerto Rico?" Baby Girl asks.

"Flying the helicopter for the search and rescue team in Yellowstone?" I offer. "Or diving for buried treasure in a pirate ship recently found off the coast of North Carolina. And she plans to donate all the money to cancer research."

"Working at a diner in the desert, somewhere along Route 66, and wearing a name tag that says 'Velma,'" Baby Girl says, excited. "But really she's incognito, working for the government on a top-secret mission."

"As an alien hunter," I say. "And the diner is actually a science laboratory."

"What are they studying?"

"Love," I say. "Humans never seem to get it right."

"No, we don't," Baby Girl says.

"What does Buddhism say about love?"

"That falling in love is a returning home."

I'm not sure if Baby Girl is telling the truth, considering she hasn't quoted a single person accurately . . . ever. But I dare to ask, "What does that mean?"

"Love is a mirror. A reminder that it exists in us always."

"Most days when I look in the mirror, I don't like what I see," I say.

"If love was easy to see, we wouldn't be lonely right now," Baby Girl says. "Yogananda said that."

"Who's Yogananda?"

"Does it matter?" Baby Girl smiles wearily. "Do you want me to curl your hair for your date-date?"

"No, thanks."

"We could practice kissing with a pillow." When I turn down the offer, Baby Girl says, "I'm not sure I'm cut out to be your sister."

I tell her that most of the time, Lizzie was just *there*. That words don't matter as much as presence does. Sometimes we just need people to occupy space for us.

Baby Girl takes my hand and walks me over to the mirror.

"Just so you know, I like what I see," she says, and because Baby Girl is looking at me and not at herself, I'm pretty sure she's telling the truth. "So what are you going to wear tonight?"

"I think the only choice is to be myself."

Baby Girl leaves me standing at the mirror, where I'm staring at my reflection. I narrow my eyes, searching the girl before me.

This is me.

I'm left with two options: hope there's more to me, something unseen that's waiting to come out, or fear that this is it, that all I'll ever be is standing in front of me, already here.

17

CHEROPHOBIC

Luca should be here soon. I'm back on the roof, eyes on the sky above, but really I'm trying not to worry about what might happen on earth tonight. Dusk has just begun. Slowly the stars will appear, one at a time, each taking its turn lighting the night.

A text comes through to my phone.

Wilder: Some people have an actual fear of happiness

His bedroom light turns on.

Wilder: It's called cherophobia

Wilder: They think joy is always followed by sadness

Isn't it, I think. Happiness never lasts. Sadness finds a way to seep into the cracks, waiting until the right time to freeze and break everything apart.

Me: Is there a cure?

Wilder: Yeah do happy things

Me: Sounds easy enough

Wilder: IDK

Wilder: Sometimes happiness is hard to find

A star ignites above me.

Wilder: What's it like out there?

So I tell him. The air temperature is perfect—not too hot, but not cold. I smell wet grass from this afternoon's rainstorm. A breeze rustles the trees. I tell him how, from up here, if I close my eyes, it feels like I'm floating.

Wilder: Are u happy now?

Me: Actually I think I might be cherophobic

Wilder: At least u know the cure

Me: I'm scared tho

Wilder: You could stay inside

Wilder: With me

I take a deep breath.

Me: But then I wouldn't smell the rain

Me: Are u still thinking about opening the window?

Wilder: Sometimes but if I open it something is bound to change

Wilder: What if it makes me worse?

Wilder: I'm used to this life

Another star lights the sky. A flip of a switch.
From down the street I hear a skateboard rolling over pavement, and the very next moment, Luca stands at the foot of my driveway.

Me: What if it makes u better?

18

TAKE THE PLUNGE

Luca wears a pair of black jeans with tears in the knees, a white T-shirt, and his well-worn black-and-white-checkered Vans, skateboard in hand. He looks wild and unkempt, his hair a mess, his nose ring somehow more pronounced in the fading light of day.

I can't take my eyes off him.

"You should probably know that my dad's a cop," I say from my perch. "He's killed people before."

"Wicked."

"He taught me how to put someone in a headlock. And I've done it. He passed out."

"Hot. Promise to show me later?" Luca's eyes sparkle, like stars fell to the earth and live inside him. It's distracting. My defenses are weakening.

"I don't put out. I've never kissed anybody, and I'm probably pretty bad at it, so if you think this is a 'get drunk and have sex' date, you're wrong."

"I didn't know that was an option."

"It's not."

"And who says I want to kiss you?" Luca asks.

"You don't?"

"No. I totally do." He smiles. "Trick question. Now, will you please come down?"

"I'm not done yet. I'm a total loser. I don't have any friends, so if you think I'm some popular girl who will be good for your reputation, I won't. I'll probably ruin it."

"And I told you I'm a failure, so it sounds like we're perfect for each other. Plus, we don't even go to the same school."

Luca gazes up at me, his smile never wavering.

"Are you done yet?" he asks. "Anything else you want to tell me?"

"I have bad breath in the morning."

"Everyone does."

"I can't catch a ball to save my life."

"I hate all sports with balls. Too prosaic."

"I almost failed algebra. Twice."

"I've almost failed at everything," Luca says. "Twice."

"I used to eat Play-Doh when I was a kid."

"I preferred glue."

"I hate watermelon."

"Well, now you've done it," he says. But he doesn't move.

"My second toe is way longer than my first. I have two different-sized thumbs and an outie belly button."

"You are trying to turn me off? Because I am squarely *on* right now. Keep talking about toes."

I groan. Luca will find something wrong and leave, just like everyone else. If I can just expose exactly what it is now, we can skip the date and get straight to the leaving. It'll hurt less.

"I trip all the time. I cry at Christmas commercials, and I hate video games." I'm grasping.

"You don't think I cry at Christmas commercials, too?" he asks. "The one with the neighbor who watches the old woman across the street, checking her mailbox every day for a Christmas card, but she never finds one? And then the neighbor sends a card, and the old woman cries?" Luca pretends to weep. His fake crying has me giggling, feeling a lightness in my chest, like maybe a date with him is exactly what I need. But one glance at the ground reminds me how badly the fall will hurt.

"I have cherophobia," I say seriously.

"I don't know what that is, but don't worry, we'll use protection. Are you done yet?"

What I want to say is, *I'm scared. I'm scared. I'm scared.* What I really say is, "Why me?"

"Wren." He says my name like he's desperate to utter it. "Why not you?"

Then Luca lifts his hand up toward me, his palm open. "Now, please come down."

I steal a glance at Wilder's window. There are so many more things I could tell Luca that might send him packing, before we ever get close, but a breeze brings the scent of summer rain back. Do I really want to hide and live without *this*?

"Or if you prefer, I'll just come up there," Luca says.

He makes for the ladder, and I holler, "Fine! I'm coming down."

He meets me at the bottom, his figure towering over mine, his body so close that I almost think we might be made of the same substance. That maybe I'm not so different after all, because he is familiar. Like I knew him, even before I did.

"So . . . your dad's a cop. That's good to know. Is he home?"

"Not at the moment."

Luca appears relieved. "Maybe don't tell him my last name."

"What's your last name?"

"Lowry."

"Do you have a record or something?"

"I like to consider it more of a scrapbook," he says. "But don't worry. All minor offenses."

"What kind of offenses?"

But Luca won't budge. "You can trust me, Wren."

"My dad taught me not to trust criminals."

"'Criminal' sounds like too harsh a word. I prefer 'delinquent youth with a propensity for trespassing.' Do you always do what your dad tells you to do?"

Before Lizzie left, yes. But now . . .

He smirks at my lack of response and reveals a pair of roller skates from his backpack.

"Put these on," he says.

"No way. I told you: I don't know how to roller-skate. And I trip all the time. I have terrible balance. I can't even do a handstand. I'll die, and then my dad will kill you for killing me. It'll be a double homicide. I can't risk it."

My cherophobia is really spiking.

Luca cups my cheeks with his hands, stepping so close I think he might lean down and kiss me right here, right now, in my driveway. Thank God, Chief is at work. My breath catches in my throat. Luca touches me so easily, I almost think I'm real and whole and completely visible.

"Just because you don't know how to do something," Luca says, "doesn't mean you shouldn't try it."

"I'm pretty sure that's the opposite of what they teach us in health class."

"I've always preferred the education offered in the real world."

"Is that why you skip school?"

"Who said I skip school?"

"Leia."

Luca releases my face from his grasp. "It's not natural to sit at a desk all day. Humans are nomadic at our core. We're meant to move."

That's what I'm afraid of, I think.

"I'm not very good at moving," I say.

"Lucky for you, I'm an expert at it. I'll help you."

"But—"

Luca's finger comes to my lips, quieting me. "Don't say it."

We don't move. Our eyes connect, as if we're both acknowledging that we're touching.

I step back.

"OK."

"OK," he echoes. "Take off your shoes."

I do as Luca requests. He crouches down in front of me and slides each skate on, then ties the laces.

My stomach sits in my throat, clogging it with anxiety, and I haven't even stood up yet.

Luca puts my shoes in his backpack. "Take my hands, Wren."

I read once that babies are born with the reflex to grab. If a person presses her finger into the palm of an infant, the baby will grasp it unconditionally. We're born to hold on to other human beings with all our might. Yet somewhere along the way, we lose that instinct. We let go. We grow suspicious and wary. Worry overrides instinct. Instead of believing that love is the intention of a hand placed into our palm, we convince ourselves we're being fooled. We don't deserve it.

Maybe the entire world is full of cherophobics.

"I won't let you fall," Luca assures me. "But you have to take my hands."

My fingers gently slide along his palms, taking their time to feel the lines etched into his skin. I don't know Luca's story, but I'm pretty sure if my hand stayed in his for long enough, he'd tell me.

From this moment forward there is no going back. Forward is all I have.

With his backpack on, skateboard latched to it, Luca helps me move. I wobble, rolling chaotically, my balance challenged. My feet come out from underneath me, and I'm propelled backward. I let go of his hands and grab for air instead, but Luca's reflexes are fast, and his arms are around my waist before I fall. He pulls me to his chest.

"You weren't kidding," he says. "You do have terrible balance."

"I wasn't lying about any of it. I have weird toes, too. Should we end the date now?"

"Say 'toes' again."

"Toes."

Luca moans. "God, you're hot."

"I'm serious."

"So am I." He places me back on my feet and takes my hands again.

"What do I do now?" I ask.

"Bend your knees. Keep your weight centered."

I do as he says. Luca pulls me down the driveway and into the street.

"What if a car comes?"

"No more what-ifs."

"But what if—"

Luca stops. "I won't let a car hit you."

I stare at my feet.

"Eyes up. If you look down at your feet, you're more likely to fall. You have to keep your eyes in front of you. Trust that your feet will adjust to what you see. Eyes down and you see things too late."

"OK."

We start down the street, Luca pulling me as I wobble.

"You know a lot about this," I say. "How long have you been skateboarding?"

"Feels like my whole life. It's the only thing I've ever been good at."

"I don't believe you."

"You should see my report card. You'd believe me then. My parents are so proud," he says sarcastically. "They brag about me all the time."

He attempts a smile, but it's laced with a touch of dejection. "There's always one fuck-up in every family, right?"

I think of Lizzie. She and Luca are so similar, but I would never call her *that*. She is so much more.

"You're not a fuck-up, Luca."

He cracks for a moment before the veneer of carelessness coats him again.

"Enough about me," he says. "Tell me about your family."

"There's not much to tell."

"You're lying." But he says it with a grin. "Every family has its secrets."

If he only knew about the fifth floor of the library.

"If I told you my secrets, they wouldn't be secrets anymore," I say.

"You're playing hard to get again."

"Maybe," I say with a smile that buds from a real place of happiness. "Secrets have to be earned."

Luca says, in complete seriousness, "Then I'll work hard at it."

The night air pops and sizzles between us. I've forgotten I'm on roller skates. I've forgotten to be worried. I've practically forgotten who I am.

"Are you ready to try skating on your own?" Luca asks.

The street is empty, the lights from the streetlamps illuminating our path. Am I ready? If I don't try, how will I ever know?

I release my hands from Luca's, and a satisfied grin blooms on his face.

"What do I do?"

Luca tells me to imagine I'm gliding on ice, moving back and forth, pushing with one leg at a time.

"Remember, eyes forward. Weight balanced. Bend your knees."

My body reacts to his instructions.

"Just skate down to the stop sign," he says. "I'll be right next to you."

The sign isn't that far.

"You can do this, Wren."

"Promise you won't leave my side."

And when Luca says, "I promise," I believe him.

"OK," I say, because if I don't do this, and the date ends, the regret will never wash away.

A little push, to start. A wobble, and then another wobble. My arms spread out at my sides. Eyes on the stop sign.

"That's good," Luca says. "Give it a little more. Don't be afraid of the speed. You can handle it."

But can I? All of this?

For my entire life I've worried that Lizzie would leave. I made myself responsible for it, thinking I'd lose myself if I ever lost her. But here I am. I've survived. I live. The leaving hasn't destroyed me yet.

So I push a little harder. Roll a little faster.

Didn't Leia say that being a roller girl taught her that pain is an inevitable part of progress? At what point does pain turn into something more, something that doesn't hold you back but lifts you up?

The faster I go, the harder Luca works to keep up.

"Almost there!" he hollers, the intersection approaching. "Stop at the sign!"

But he didn't tell me how to do that.

"Stop?" I scream, panicked. "How?"

"Use the toe stop!"

"What's a toe stop?"

There's no time for a lesson. Luca can't save me.

"The grass!" Luca yells. "Bail out on the grass!"

It's the only way to avoid rolling right into the intersection. I make a dive for it, leaping and clearing the curb. The wheels of my skates land on the grass and catch some friction, slowing my movement but forcing my weight forward. My arms reach for stability that isn't there. I fall hard to the ground, but I do come to a stop.

In a moment Luca is next to me. The wheels on my skates are still spinning. My head is, too. Spinning and twirling and dancing, maybe for the first time ever.

"Are you OK, Wren?" Luca asks. "Can you talk? Say something."

Laughter bubbles up from my belly, and the giggles won't stop. Lying back on the ground, I see the night sky painting everything in plum and cobalt, like the fire of the day is slowly being consumed by water, and I laugh until my stomach hurts.

Luca lies on the grass next to me and exhales.

"I've failed," he says.

The laughter finally stops, and I turn to look at him. "What?"

"I said you could trust me, and look at you. You're hurt, and it's only our first date."

I realize what he's doing. It's the same thing I do. Maybe all humans do it. We see through the lens everyone else prescribes for us, instead of the one we make on our own.

Luca can see only failure. But I won't let him.

"Luca, I felt it."

"Felt what?"

I look back up at the sky and wonder why I ever thought I could capture something so beautiful on Lizzie's walls.

"The rush," I whisper.

The night hums. The air is electric.

"So tonight's not a total disaster?" Luca asks.

Then, like an ant crawling over the grass, Luca's fingers find mine.

"Far from it," I say, squeezing his hand.

19

ON THE LEDGE OF HOPE

The parking lot of South Hill High School is empty. Luca hasn't let go of my hand since I fell.

"Here we are," he says.

"It's my school."

"I know."

"I thought you hated school."

"I do."

"Then why are we here?"

"Because schools happen to be the perfect place to practice." Luca shrugs off his backpack and unhooks his skateboard.

"Really?"

"Yep. There's a ton of open space. There are ramps. There are railings."

"Railings?" My muscles are already tired just from getting here. I'm not sure how much more practicing I can do.

"Maybe someday," Luca says, a wide grin on his face.

I sit down on the steps leading to the front doors. The lights are off inside. The place feels abandoned for the summer. Lonely, really. In two years, when I graduate, I'm pretty sure the hallways won't miss me. They won't even remember I was here.

"Why are you doing this?" I ask.

"What?"

"Teaching me how to skate."

"You said you didn't know how."

"But why does it matter? Lots of people can't roller-skate."

"Most people aren't as strong as you."

"I'm not strong." Unwilling to look Luca in the eye, I examine a scrape on my hand left from the fall.

He sits down. There's space all around us, and yet he chooses to be close to me, his leg touching mine, and I think maybe that's what love is—deciding to lean in close amid a world of endless space. It would be so much easier to back away, but I resist the urge. The intimacy of our skin touching disintegrates any logic.

"Luca," I say, absorbed in him.

"Yes, Wren?"

"Could you try not to get arrested anymore?"

"Why?"

"So my dad doesn't kill you."

"Does that mean you want to go out with me again?"

"Maybe," I say. "And you should stop skipping school."

"I'll think about it."

"Luca?"

"Yeah, Wren?"

"How does the marshmallow taste so far?"

When he looks at me, the heat between us starts to boil. "Delicious. To be honest, I'm trying to stop myself from eating the whole thing all at once. Self-control has never been my forte."

"I'm starting to think maybe too much control is overrated."

His arm rests next to mine. My heart beats wildly.

"Luca?"

"Yeah, Wren?"

"I want to see you skate," I say.

It's not that I couldn't sit here all night, the dark sky above us, my skin touching his in a way I've never touched anyone before. But in a moment that feels so extraordinary, I want to witness magic.

When Luca stands, the separation of our bodies feels like Velcro pulling apart.

But as I watch him skate around the parking lot, I'm so full I can't remember what empty feels like. And maybe it will last only a moment, maybe it's as fleeting as the wind, but sometimes a moment locked in memory is all a person needs.

I knew this could happen. The needing. The wanting. But I can't look away, because from this moment into infinity, I'll know what I'd be missing.

The rush is worth the tailspin.

Watching Luca swim through air—ebbing and flowing, bending and soaring, free of restraint and completely in control of where he's going—I want him more than I've wanted anything in my life.

I want to melt into him. I want to fly with him, next to him, wrapped in him, as if gravity doesn't matter, as if flying really is possible. As if lost love can appear from nothing and walk back into my life, illuminating even the darkest of ravines and shining a light on the way out.

I just need to catch him.

I wobble only a little when I stand up. My muscles are already screaming at me to stop. The scrapes on my hands ache. Tomorrow my entire body will most likely be riddled with pain.

But I don't care.

"Don't look down," I say to myself. "Look forward."

My body is now more accustomed to the feeling of being on wheels. With less effort this time, I get myself moving. Luca is lost in the maze of ramps and sidewalks that connects all the buildings of South Hill High.

I have to find him. I skate through areas I've never noticed before—the outdoor picnic area where Jay and Chloe eat lunch when the sun is out, the football stadium's parking lot, through the quad where big pine trees shade students napping and studying.

All are empty tonight.

I come around the corner to find the cadmium yellow of the sun streaking through the night. Luca is at the top of a ramp. He catches speed, like dawn light rolling down a hill.

The ramp is steep, and I still haven't mastered how to stop, but none of this prevents me from chasing Luca.

I yell his name, and so much adrenaline is pumping through me I feel practically invincible.

He finds me at the top of the ramp, our eyes locking only briefly.

My skates pick up speed. Luca's expression reminds me of the drop I feel in my stomach as I realize I've abandoned any control. My body feels heavy as it's pulled down by gravity. The slope only makes it worse, the roller skates picking up momentum. This time there's no grass to fall into. No soft landing.

All control is lost. Hope is all that remains.

20

MOON-STAINED

Lizzie went through phases where she refused to sleep for days on end. It started when she was little. No amount of begging or pleading would force her eyes closed.

"It's just so dark sometimes, Songbird," she said once. "I don't like the darkness."

"But the night is always dark," I said.

"Not when I can see the stars. There are more suns out at night than during the day. I just need the clouds to pass."

But at times Spokane lives under a blanket of clouds for days on end.

"We should tell Chief," I begged her. "He'll know what to do."

"No." Lizzie was adamant. "He's too quick to put people in handcuffs."

"But you need sleep," I said.

"The moon never rests. It's constantly changing. Can't I be like the moon?"

I saw bags under her eyes, fatigue in her beautiful features.

"The moon is a flashlight, so shadows play on earth instead of in minds. But the clouds are blocking the moon. They need a place to play, Songbird." Lizzie's body hung heavy.

This was two years ago. Lizzie was the worst I'd ever seen.

"Please, Lizzie," I begged. "Just a little sleep."

"Have you ever noticed that it's never truly dark unless you close your eyes?" she said. "If I can just keep mine open, it won't happen again."

"What won't happen?"

"Things creep around in the darkness."

"What things?"

"Things I can't control." We were in her room on the empty floor. Olga was downstairs, asleep, and Chief was at work, helping other people survive. "With my eyes open, I can imagine anything. But when they're closed, the darkness makes its own story and I can't find the truth."

Lizzie looked at me with this helpless, tired expression I'll never forget.

"Let's go sit outside," I said. "You'll feel better with fresh air."

And so we did.

We spread out on the ground in our backyard, and slowly the clouds parted. The moon came out again, and she relaxed.

"You're moon-stained, Songbird. The night looks good on you," Lizzie said, a smile returning to her face. "If I could, I'd never sleep again. I'd keep my eyes on the moon and make sure the shadows knew I was watching them. Shadows play on the light."

Only then, with the moonlit night blanketing her body, did Lizzie finally close her eyes and sleep, as if her world was back in working order.

When we woke up the next day, covered in early-morning dew, Lizzie was back to herself. She made me promise not to tell Chief what had happened.

"He thinks I'm broken, Songbird. He wants to put me back together how *he* wants me to be. Not how I am. I can't let that happen."

I'm lost in the memory of it, swimming through it, breathing it, smelling the grass that lingered in our hair, feeling the soft dew on my skin from the sunrise, the wave of relief I felt when Lizzie turned her rested face toward mine and said, "Do you hear them? The songbirds are calling for you. They want you to come home." Lizzie grasped my hand. "I'll miss you so much when you leave, but I understand. The wilderness will call us both back to her. We can't live among the painted trees forever. But it's OK, Songbird. When you decide to fly from here, I'll kiss you goodbye and let you go."

But she left me first, with nothing but a breeze in her wake to kiss my cheek goodbye.

The cool night air tickles my skin as the pine trees that surround the high school catch shadows from the moonlight. I don't know what Lizzie saw when she closed her eyes. She was in an untouchable, unspeakable place I could never reach.

But tonight it's Luca, moon-stained and beautiful, who hovers over me, his aura mixing with the light of the moon, the halo around his black hair touched by twilight. So tangible.

For a moment the feeling that's consumed me for a month comes back. My body is adrift. Emptiness leaves room for the echo of sadness. But I'm not so hollow anymore.

Luca fills the night with my name.

Wren.

Wren.

Wren.

It's as if he's pushing life into my lungs, soothing the claustrophobic ache in my chest. Filling me. Lizzie's hand dissolves, and the memory of her whisks away into the night and becomes speckles of stars above.

"Wren, can you hear me?"

Luca, can you save me? Keep pulling, I urge him. *Keep breathing. Don't leave me in the ravine.*

"Wren, talk to me."

"You're a love seat," I say.

"What?"

"You're a love seat."

"I think you're concussed."

"If I had to categorize you as a piece of furniture, you'd be a love seat." Luca grins deviously. "Well, you can sit on me anytime you want."

"I should warn you. I'm a chair that's missing a leg. Wobbly at best. At worst, disposable."

"Don't worry. I'll hold you up."

I'm jealous of the moon's touch on his shoulder and hair and lips. Luca sits me up, slowly, cautiously.

"Do I need to call an ambulance?" he asks.

"No."

"But you blacked out for a second," Luca says.

He doesn't understand that my life has been a blackout for the past month. Maybe longer.

"If you call an ambulance, my dad will come, and then he'll ask what your last name is, and I'll never be allowed to see you again."

Luca freezes. "OK. No ambulance."

His hand feels the back of my head. I wince slightly.

"I need to check you out, Wren," he says. "Make sure you're OK. Hold still and tell me if it hurts."

I can't explain to him that this is nothing. The pain of falling is easily handled. It's the heart that's not so simple.

Luca starts with my feet, taking one skate off at a time. "Any pain?" he asks.

I shake my head.

A smirk pulls at his cheeks, and he touches my longer second toe. "You weren't lying. That toe *is* long."

His hands move to my legs, inspecting every inch, his thumb moving smoothly over my skin.

I bite down hard.

"Does that hurt?" He backs up.

"No." I'm resisting the urge to grab him and not let go.

"You might be the toughest person I know," Luca says.

"I don't feel strong."

"You just wiped out, blacked out, and told me you're fine," Luca says incredulously. "What more proof do you need?" His fingers are back, searching my skin inch by inch, just like he promised.

"Well, in that case, you should know you're not a failure, Luca."

He blows off my comment with a sarcastic grunt. "What would you call tonight?"

"Magic."

Our eyes connect. He searches my face, as if the truth might be carved in the creases around my eyes when I smile.

You can do it, Songbird, Lizzie said.

The list of reasons I could never do a handstand was long—my arms weren't strong enough, my legs too heavy, the ground too hard, my life too broken for the extraordinary.

I'm dead weight, I thought. *Baggage. Heavy. Unwanted even by the air. It'll drop me.*

I just know I can't do it, I said to her.

Then borrow my belief for a while, Lizzie said.

Instead I borrowed everything else—her life, her breath, her world—and left whoever I was behind. My belief in Lizzie was enough. She's the wire I've clung to for stability. I've pretended for so long, I don't know the difference between real and fantasy—the girl Lizzie created and believed me to be, and the girl I actually am.

"What if I disappoint you?" I ask Luca.

"What if *I* disappoint you?" he replies.

"I guess we'll just have to borrow each other's belief until we find it in ourselves," I say to him. "You can borrow my belief in you."

"You can borrow mine, too," he says. "Now, hold still."

Luca moves his attention to my hands, my arms, my shoulders, his hands not leaving a single exposed inch of me without his touch.

"Almost done," he says. "I just need to check your head one more time."

Luca is before me, his eyes on mine, his lips so close when he speaks that his words travel from inside him to inside me and pass only briefly through the night air, with no time to cool.

His fingers tangle in my hair, from the nape of my neck to the crown of my head, soft and searching. If there was any pain, Luca has eased it with his fingers and the humble touch of acknowledgment.

"From now on, no skating without a helmet," he says. "But I think you're OK."

Thinking is impossible right now. All I can do is feel.

"Are you sure you've checked everywhere?" I ask, sitting forward. Closing the space between us.

The air is magnetic, the moonbeams charged with vibration.

"Maybe not everywhere," he whispers.

He leans in, hands still tangled in my hair, our breath swirling together. Lips an inch apart.

But the ringing of a phone startles the night. Luca pulls back from me.

"Damn." He gets his phone from his pocket. "Fuck."

"What is it?"

Luca stands. Cold circulates around us. He walks away from me to answer the phone. I can catch only bits and pieces of what he says.

"Hello?" A pause. "At the high school." Another. "Just skateboarding." And then in a clipped voice, "No, I'm not doing anything stupid." More space, more distance. "I didn't . . . OK, OK. I'll be right there." One more pause. Luca's shoulders fall. "I'm sorry."

He shoves his phone back in his pocket.

"I have to go," he says.

"Is everything OK?"

"It's fine." He runs his hands through his hair. "Actually, it's not fine."

"Can I help?" I ask.

"No." He says it so quickly, the word feels like a slap. He pauses for a weighted breath that pulls his chest down. "I'm sorry."

Inch by inch, space invades the night. Luca gets my shoes from his backpack and sets them on the bench. The heat between us is gone. I'm desperate for its return. I'm a period begging an ellipsis to stay.

"This isn't how I wanted tonight to go," Luca says. He's dressed in disappointment. A text dings on his phone. With a frustrated grunt, his entire body tenses.

"It's OK," I say. "I can make it home. It's not far."

"I don't want to leave you, but . . ."

But he has to. That's what Luca doesn't want to say.

He moves closer. For a moment the space between us is gone. Luca says, "Just promise me you won't hurt yourself going home."

"I promise."

And before I know it, he is gone. Lost in the night.

With shoes on my feet, my legs feel extra heavy. It takes effort to walk home, as if my feet are dragging, drudging their way back.

The skates are slung over my shoulder, saved for the next time someone pulls me down from my perch, offers me a hand, and lets me borrow their strength.

Bouquet of Sunflowers, 1881

Dear Songbird,

I've decided Monet was a complete daredevil to paint like he did. He might be the bravest man who ever lived. I know he didn't jump in front of bullets and save children from burning buildings, like Chief does.

He simply painted outside the lines and started a revolution.

I love you,

Lizzie

Wren Plumley
20080 21st Ave.
Spokane, WA 99203

21

GONE MISSING

I don't remember moving from Boise. I don't remember the house I was brought home to from the hospital, or my nursery, or even my mother's face in the flesh. Any knowledge that I have comes from Lizzie.

Stored deep in the basement are pictures of our mom, but they're covered in spiders and darkness. I've never had the courage to go down there and find them. I think Chief wanted it that way when he put them there.

Lizzie made the journey to that part of the basement only once, unbeknownst to Chief. He banned us from that part of the house, but by putting a wall in front of Lizzie, he was just asking for her to make a rope out of curiosity. Once she threw it over the wall, Lizzie was going to climb.

When she returned from the darkness of the basement, her cheeks were stained with tears and she was clutching a photo.

"Don't look, Songbird," Lizzie said. "Just trust me. In some places, make-believe isn't possible."

So I never looked at the pictures.

After that the basement was off limits. Chief's invisible wall was strongly in place. Lizzie and I stayed aboveground, where vines could turn into swings and flowers were transformed into tiaras. Where it was easier to pretend in the sun than remember in the darkness.

I don't know what Lizzie did with the pictures of our mom. I trusted that she took care of them, like she took care of me. I didn't want to see them. I knew our mom didn't look like me. I can tell because of Chief. Sometimes he looked at Lizzie with this pain in his eyes, like his heart was breaking just at the sight of her, and I knew he missed our mom to the point he couldn't breathe. And then Chief would make a list or go to the gym or save the life of a person who, just like him, wasn't sure he or she wanted to be saved.

Lizzie must be a replica of our mom.

But some memories you can't walk out of. Some are so ingrained in the fiber of your being, you can't hide from them or change them. All a person can do is live with the haunting.

I was four years old when Aunt Betsy and Uncle Kirk came to Spokane for Thanksgiving. Every now and then the image of them comes to me. Chief and Betsy sitting on our couch, Kirk in the armchair, a beer in his hand, football on TV in the background.

"She couldn't bring herself to hold her," Chief said as I hid behind them with a stomachache from eating too much. "It was as if Wren was . . . repellent. How could a baby be untouchable?"

"Stop blaming yourself," Betsy said. "Vivienne made her choices."

"It's been two years," Kirk added. "The past is the past. You can't change it."

"I'll never stop blaming myself," Chief said. "It was my idea to have a second child. I was set on it. I thought it would help. If Wren was never born . . ."

Aunt Betsy embraced Chief in a loving hug as I stayed hiding and, my feet cold on the wood floor, tried to catch their warmth and felt even more sick to my stomach.

If a mother finds her child repellent, what's to say the world wants that child anymore?

Lizzie could never understand my struggle, because *she* was wanted. Everyone felt it. Even the trees begged for her weight to dangle from their branches.

But an untouchable child wonders if she's destined to walk alone, if she's a mistake dragged behind her parents, bumping along the road until, piece by piece, she is reduced to nothing.

Was it even worth trying to hold myself up? Hold myself together? Was *I* worth it?

How did my mother know I was repellent? Could she smell it on me? Taste it in the kisses she left on my cheek? Feel it in the heat that passed between us?

Did I cry for her? Did she plug her ears? Did Chief have to feed me bottles and rock me to sleep because my mom couldn't bring herself to?

Did she take one look at me and know, deep in her heart, that it would be impossible to ever love me? To even pretend? Did she leave me before I was even born?

In some places, make-believe isn't possible.

My problem with handstands is that I can't get the courage to jump. I don't trust what will happen when I let go. I don't trust myself to handle it. To toss the world upside down by choice. To let the pieces fall away until I'm stripped down to my core.

Instead, for years, I sat perched on the roof, watching life below and silently asking the birds to come and take me home.

It never occurred to me that the world can flip on a person when her feet are solidly planted on the ground. Life hits a bump, and suddenly everything is tossed into the air.

But memories are like a sponge—incomplete, filled with holes, and yet so absorbent, they can consume a person. Still, we decide what to fill those holes with. I've given my memories power. Fueled them. Burned and branded them into my brain, making their mark permanent. Because the truth is, there's safety in being repellent. Untouchable. Invisible.

But then Luca put his hand in mine and said, "Come with me," and now everything is different.

I'm looking for a research paper about woodpeckers," I say to the librarian. "I believe it's called *When Instinct Goes Wrong: An Investigation of Woodpeckers and Their Relationship with Wood.*"

The librarian types on her computer and then says, "It's been checked out."

"It has?"

She nods. "And it looks like it should have been returned weeks ago." She gives me an apologetic look. "I hate to say it, but usually when books go missing for this long, we don't get them back."

"So it's lost?"

"Most likely. But if you want to give me your email address, I can email you if it turns up."

"That's OK," I say. "I guess all secrets eventually come out."

The night is quiet again. I woke up and everything hurt today. But not how I thought it would. It hurts to breathe and move and be, because I'm more alive today than I was yesterday.

With my bedroom window open, I sit on the sill, feeling the ache everywhere and hoping it stays. Chief wouldn't like me sitting so close to the edge, but he's not home to tell me otherwise.

Me: Someone took a secret of mine

Wilder: What are u going to do?

Me: IDK what are my options?

Wilder: You could go search for it

Me: I have Driver's Ed and my dad's on graveyard shift all week

Wilder: You could wait for it to be returned

Me: There's no guarantee it will be

Me: And I think I've been waiting too much lately

The scrapes on my hands ache. Wilder paces his bedroom. I watch him move in and out of the window frame. There one minute, gone the next. But I'm also watching my driveway. Like maybe Luca will show up at any second—backpack on, soaring on his skateboard—to call me down again.

But the night remains quiet.

Me: I have an idea but it's kind of crazy

Wilder: What?

Me: I could just let my secret go

Wilder: Could u really do that?

Me: Maybe

Wilder: But what about the person who took it?

Wilder: They know the truth about u

Me: The truth changes all the time

Me: They can have my secret

Wilder: Doesn't that scare u?

Me: Secrets only have power when they're secrets

Me: But once u let them go . . .

Wilder disappears from the window. The light in his room is still on. My phone goes dark. Minutes pass. Somewhere in the distant night a car honks its horn. The longer Wilder is missing, the more I start to panic, thinking he's fainted or collapsed. Or gone.

Me: Wilder?

Wilder: I'm here

Wilder: I just feel a little faded today

My panic settles.

Me: OK I only have one more question

Wilder: What?

Me: What if I really am cursed?

The pause echoes in the night as I wait for Wilder's response to appear on my phone. He doesn't come back to the window.

Wilder: I think the better question is

Wilder: What if ur not?

With that, his bedroom light goes out.

22

A VACANT ROOM

Baby Girl has definitively decided that by the time she goes to Spokane Community College in a month, she will know who she is. The countdown is on. She's on a scavenger hunt for herself. And today we are searching for clues in Target.

"Anything a person could want is in this store. I've got to be hiding in here somewhere. Let's look in the bathroom section."

"What are we looking for exactly?"

"Me."

"How will you know when we've found . . . you?"

"Shakespeare once said, 'To be or not to be me. In the end, we are what we buy.'"

"That's not how *Hamlet* goes."

"Who said anything about *Hamlet*? Come on."

I wish my heart was into helping her, but I'm consumed with Luca. His eyes. His lips. His hands. And I'm not sure the past should occupy our house as much as it currently does. It might need to move out soon to make room for the present.

Luca hasn't come back to Driver's Ed. I waited, pulling his usual desk extra close to mine, waiting for the moment he would coast through the door and take up the air with his scent.

But he hasn't showed all week. Frustration settled around me. Where was he? Did he decide to give up? To stop coming? Just like that? Like he does with high school.

He wants me to believe I'm strong, but what about him? If he's willing to quit, why should I be any different?

I shouldn't let doubt creep up on me like the cold chill of a familiar ghost. But the more I replay the night, the harder it becomes to fight the uncertainty of reality. Maybe I made it all up. Maybe it was all a trick of hands and shadows and moonlight. Maybe it was easier than I thought for Luca to let me go.

"This is all plastic junk." Baby Girl can't find anything in Target that gives her a clue as to who she is. "'We are merely machines for soul-sucking corporations who use our labor and shit on our individuality.' Carl Jung said that. Let's go to Starbucks."

But Starbucks only makes it worse.

I'm so consumed with my own problems that it isn't until we're about to order that I see complete panic on Baby Girl's face.

"What is it?"

Paralyzed, Baby Girl looks at me. "I don't know if I can do this."

"What do you mean? Drink coffee? Just get decaf."

"*Order* coffee."

"You've ordered coffee before. What do you like?"

"That's the problem," she says. "I've never ordered for *myself*. I order what I *think* I should get. I ask myself, 'What would a pothead order?' A Caramel Cocoa Cluster Frappuccino with extra whipped cream, of course. Or a theater geek? A double Americano with a side of angst, and don't get me started on Samuel Beckett or how Lin-Manuel Miranda has single-handedly revived Broadway. A serious book nerd? Endless black coffee, preferably burnt, and served in a mug with cats on it. But *me*? The real me? I have no idea. I think I need to sit down."

Baby Girl practically falls into a chair, defeated.

"If I can't pick a coffee drink, how will I ever pick a major? And if I can't pick a major, I'll never graduate college, and if I never graduate, I won't get a job, and if I don't have a job, I have to live at home for the rest of my life. In my mother's basement."

"Plenty of people don't go to college." I sit down across from her.

"That's not the point," she says. "Life is a bunch of stacked dominos, Wren. If I don't find out who I am soon, they're going to start falling, and I won't be able to stop it." She puts her head down on the table. "Why is this so hard?"

I think what Baby Girl really wants to know is what could have been so wrong with her that someone, her dad, felt the need to change how she looked on the outside with his fists and hands.

"He didn't show up," she says. "Every month, my dad and I meet at the same stupid Denny's and order the same stupid meal and have the same stupid conversation, and at the end he gives me the same stupid wad of cash and we leave. That's the routine. And every time I tell myself that I won't do it again next month. I don't care about his money. Then the date rolls around, and there I am, sitting in the same filthy booth, waiting for him." Baby Girl looks at me with this completely cracked stare that opens a wound in her soul. It radiates to the surface of her brown eyes. "*I* was supposed to leave first. *I* was supposed to disappoint *him*. Not the other way around. I was supposed to push over the first domino. But I never had the guts to do it. Why did he get the guts and I didn't? He's officially taken everything from me. What do I do now?"

When I painted the first tree on Lizzie's blank wall, she sat on her floor and watched me with this look of complete awe on her face. "All it takes is a brushstroke, Songbird, and an artist opens a new world.

You have magic in your hands, and you don't even realize it. Paint me a world to believe in. One brushstroke at a time."

So I say to Baby Girl, "Let's just paint a brushstroke today and see what happens."

I order a taster of every drink Starbucks has to offer, much to the chagrin of the barista, who pouts and huffs. But this is life or falling dominos. So we begin to paint Baby Girl, one brushstroke at a time.

And I do my best not to think about Luca, how he's knocked me over like a domino and there's no going back.

Chloe and Jordan Hoffer, another popular junior girl, walk in the door. It's been weeks since I've seen Chloe, and she gives me a deer-in-headlights look before ignoring the eye contact and talking to Jordan, who, half listening and texting, is completely oblivious to my existence.

Baby Girl is deep into the little cups on the table, so she doesn't feel the awkward energy in the room. But to me it's heavy and thick. And it smells of the past. Of strawberry lip gloss and late-night popcorn.

The truth is that no one is pure evil. But remembering the good parts of a person makes it hurt more, because that's when hope shows up.

Hope that love was written somewhere in my story line with Chloe.

Hope is the reason Baby Girl sat in a filthy booth at Denny's, waiting for a man who *might* love her.

Baby Girl is halfway through her nearly thirty drinks. So far she's liked the chai-tea latte and strawberry smoothie.

"I need to go to the bathroom," I say.

"Brilliant. I'm so buzzed right now, my heart might explode. Can that happen?"

"I don't think so."

"Good." She takes down a skinny mocha in one gulp. "I'd hate to die before I truly know myself."

After a few minutes I'm forced out of hiding in the bathroom, only to find Chloe waiting outside the door. She pulls me into the corner, all inconspicuous-like.

"You're hanging out with Baby Girl now?"

"Why do you care?"

"She's weird, Wren."

"So what?"

"So, she shaved her head."

"I like it."

Chloe groans. "I can't save you from everything all the time."

"If this is you trying to save me, remind me not to hire you as a lifeguard."

"You're committing social suicide."

"You can't commit social suicide when you aren't social to begin with," I say. "And I'm not the one headed to the guillotine."

"What does that mean?"

"All I'm saying is Anne Boleyn's last words were, 'Turns out he wasn't worth it.'"

"You just don't understand," Chloe says.

"Then explain it to me." But what I'm really thinking is, *Give me hope that love exists here.*

"You've never dated anyone, Wren. Jay needs me. I'm sorry if that makes you mad."

I start to walk away. "Forget it."

Chloe is just like her mom, all backhanded apologies and contradictions. Rehashing this with Chloe is like picking broken pieces of a relationship out of a garbage can that stinks of old bananas.

"I was always second best," she blurts out. "And I got sick of it, OK? You and Lizzie lived in your own little world, and there was never enough room for me. Well, now you know what it feels like. I finally found someone who puts me first. There isn't room for you in my life right now. That's just how it goes with love. Sometimes you have to kick people out to make room for something better. You did it to me, and now I'm doing it to you."

"Chloe!" Jordan hollers to her. "Let's go!"

She leaves me standing by the bathroom, and before she walks out the door, I see Jordan ask, "Who's that?"

And Chloe says, "Nobody."

I'm left to wonder if Chloe was actually telling the truth. Did I kick her out to save enough room for Lizzie? Did I do that with everyone?

I return to the table. When Baby Girl notices my quietness, she asks, "What's wrong?"

"Can you be my sister for a second?"

Baby Girl sits up straight in the seat, just how Lizzie would, this twinkle in her eye that reflects the sun, even here in Starbucks. She really imitates other people well. I hope she manages to find herself, because when she does, she's sure to shine. "How can I help?"

I tell her about Chloe and Jay and what Chloe just said to me.

"Is this all my fault?" I ask.

Baby Girl thinks and then says, "I can't answer that, but Chloe has one thing all wrong. You don't kick people out in the name of love."

"You don't?"

"Wren, I've spent the past six years visiting a man who's a complete asshole, and eating lukewarm Moons Over My Hammy once a month. Why? Because love makes you build a bigger house, even when the tenants are a complete mess."

"Who said that?"

"I did."

I think Baby Girl just painted a brushstroke.

"Just so you know, Lizzie wouldn't have said it like that. I think only you could have done that."

Baby Girl smiles genuinely, but it's fleeting.

"I still don't know what I like best." She gestures to all the empty cups.

"Maybe you're just not a coffee person."

"Maybe."

It breaks my heart to see Baby Girl's sadness.

"Maybe we should try something else," I say.

"Like what?"

"How do you feel about sandwiches?"

23

THE MORE, THE MERRIER

But Luca's not at Rosario's Market either. I'm starting to think maybe I made him up. We find Leia, and Baby Girl acknowledges her.

Leia says, "I'm going to kill Luca. That asshole didn't show up for his shift, so I had to spend the past three hours slicing deli meat that's been injected with nitrates, put through a meat grinder, congealed in a refrigerator, and sold to the public as 'natural.'"

I know Leia's real, so Luca must be real. And this realization hurts even more.

Being real sucks sometimes.

"There's nothing natural about meat that comes vacuum sealed in plastic," Leia says.

She's a new level of fiery today.

"'The world is a vacuum-sealed plastic container,'" Baby Girl proclaims loudly. "Einstein said that. Or maybe it was Newton. Or Jesus."

"I know you," Leia says to Baby Girl. "Love your hair. Or lack thereof."

"If that's the truth, can you point me in the direction of myself? I'm lost in this grocery store somewhere. Wren thought I might be hiding in the sandwiches, but it sounds like sandwiches are just hiding nitrates."

"You're weird," Leia says. "I dig weird." Today, her pin pronounces, **WE ARE ALL TEMPORARILY NOT DIRT.**

"She's on a lot of caffeine right now," I say.

Baby Girl runs a hand over her skin. "I think I might be electric."

"Can I touch your head?" Leia asks.

"Sure." Baby Girl bends down so Leia can reach.

She runs a hand over Baby Girl's shaved head. "Cool."

"Did you feel it?"

"What?"

"The electricity. Maybe I'm really a robot who thinks she's human and I'm really just wasting my time trying to find myself because my insides are just a bunch of wires and plugs."

"Go easy on yourself. All humans are robots," Leia scoffs. "Just a cog in the propaganda machine. Why do you think we started drinking cow's milk in the first place? Because the American government put tons of money into an advertising campaign to help dairy farmers, that's why. But if everyone took a second to really think about it, we'd realize we're grown people drinking cows' breast milk."

"That's gross."

"Tell me about it. Patchouli?" Leia takes the bottle from her pocket.

"Sure." Baby Girl dabs some on her hands.

"So Luca isn't here?" I say. "You haven't seen him?"

"No. And if he gets fired for missing his shift, I'm going to kick his ass." Leia cracks her knuckles. "What's going on with you two anyway?"

"Nothing," I say too quickly. Lies come easier than the truth most days, and by the look on Leia's face, she doesn't believe me. But she lets it go.

"One of the roller girls is having a party this weekend. Want to come?" she asks. "I can introduce you to the team."

"A party?" I say. "I've never actually been to one of those."

"They're usually pretty fun."

"Can I come?" Baby Girl asks. "I don't have anything going on this weekend."

"Sure," Leia says. "The more, the merrier." She is the opposite of Chloe. Open. Constantly making room. Even if the world is a vacuum-sealed plastic container, she makes the best of the space she's got. "Give me your phone."

Baby Girl and Leia exchange numbers.

"I'll pick you both up on Saturday."

Baby Girl and I leave the grocery store.

"I'm sorry you didn't find yourself today," I say.

"That's not completely true."

"Did you decide which coffee you like best?" I ask, hopeful.

"No," Baby Girl says, looking over her shoulder at Leia. "But I'm thinking I might be gay."

24

TAKE TWO

Chief is at work Saturday night, Olga is sitting on our couch watching reruns of *Keeping Up with the Kardashians*, and as I wait for Leia I'm doing crunches and push-ups—the kind my PE teacher makes us do in gym class.

"What you doing?" Olga asks.

"Working out."

"You never work out before."

A thin layer of sweat has formed on my skin. "You're messing up my counting."

Olga dismisses me. I switch to push-ups when my abs can't take the crunches anymore. But when I can barely squeak out two before falling on my face, she laughs.

"You not built for sport, Wren."

"How do you know?"

"I know." Olga eyes me. "You delicate. Sport is too dangerous. You get hurt."

"Life hurts," I mumble, picking myself off the floor. Leia pulls into the driveway and beeps.

"Where are you going?" Olga asks. Her eyes don't leave the television screen.

"Out."

"That's the second time this week. You never go out."

"Yes, I do."

"No, you don't. You sit on roof."

"Not all the time."

"Yes, all the time."

"Things change."

"Not for you."

"What's that supposed to mean?"

"Ever since I know you, you don't change. In the fourteen years I come here, I take care of you since you were baby, you never change. Always the same. No cry. You barely make a peep. You give me no problems. Eat. Sleep. Poop. Repeat. Now, Lizzie—she give me problems."

Something happens on TV that shocks Olga, and she sits forward in her seat, captivated. I think I know why she constantly watches TV—my life is too boring for her to pay attention to. I'm vapor that slowly dissolves and doesn't leave a mess. Tears start to form in my eyes.

"How do you know what I do?" I say. "All you do when you're here is watch TV and sleep."

"I been here for long time," she says. "Longer than you remember. And people see things even in their sleep." She looks at me intensely for a moment, and then, as if she's decided I'm boring, she assesses my outfit—jeans and a white shirt—and shrugs right before aiming her attention back on the screen. "I change the shit in your diapers. I know more than you think."

I have to clench my jaw and hold my heart in place. My heart is in desperate danger of falling straight to the ground and splattering there. Olga wouldn't even notice the mess, and I'd be the one to clean it up, like always.

A fight breaks out on *Keeping Up with the Kardashians*. Olga smiles. There's no way I'm about to confess my heart to a woman who finds entertainment in other people's pain.

And the truth is, I blame Olga. She was sleeping on the couch the night Lizzie left. She was supposed to be watching us. It was her only job, and she failed.

"If that's the case, if you see things even in your sleep, then *you* let her go," I say pointedly.

Olga turns from the television screen. It's hard to imagine this tough woman ever changing my diapers or cradling me as a small child, but she's been with us ever since we moved to Spokane and Chief started on the graveyard shift. Seeing the hard look in her eyes makes me feel vacant and cold. How many nights did Olga stay on the couch and let me shiver in my room instead of offering me an extra blanket?

"No," she says. "No one could have stopped your sister."

My cheeks burn with anger. An anger that might be misplaced, but my heart is heavy today. It's been four days since my date with Luca, and still no word from him. It's amazing how much even nothing weighs on a person. So much I might break.

And I'm mad that nothing changes. That Olga thinks I'm predictable. That she thinks I'm weak and delicate. That it was always Lizzie who would leave, but never me. That Olga knew and did nothing to stop it. That Chief knew and did nothing. That I knew and put my faith in hope instead of fear.

"Do you even care?" I say. "We're just a job to you." Olga offers no response. "Chief should have fired you."

If my words have any effect on her, she doesn't show it. I can't stay inside with her any longer.

"He know it's not my fault," Olga says, turning back to the television screen as I walk out the front door. "Be home by eleven, or I tell your dad."

Leia picks me up in this old beat-up blue truck with a bumper sticker that says, **BEET IT.** The air-conditioning doesn't work, the seats are duct-taped together, and there's a weird smell coming from the vents. The car is so completely Leia. It's authentic and recycled and odd. I can't help but wonder what kind of car I am. I think I'm the police cruiser Chief bought ten years ago and that's been parked in the driveway ever since, just waiting to be driven. But lately I'm sick of being stalled.

I miss Luca. My muscles don't hurt as much anymore. I want the ache back.

The Valley, Spokane's largest suburb, is east of the city, on the way to Idaho. Leia parks in front of a large house on a street that's filled with other large houses and big lawns and SUVs and people gone on summer vacation to places like Sandpoint and Vancouver, BC. We are most definitely in the suburbs.

We stand in front of a house that's lined with perfect magenta flowers and a tightly mowed parakeet-green lawn. From the front, no one would know a party was raging inside, except for the slight thumping of bass.

All I can think about is Olga.

You don't change. Always the same. You delicate.

I want to scream.

"The burbs creep me out," Leia says.

"Why?" Baby Girl asks.

"You know what hides under manicured nails?" Leia gestures to the flowers.

"What?"

"Dirt."

They exchange warm stares that speak of something more. "I don't mind getting a little dirty," Baby Girl says.

"Me neither. As long as it's organic." Leia winks.

Baby Girl says, "I'm in the process of cleaning out the bad stuff in my life. I'm not there yet. Can you wait?"

Leia runs a hand over Baby Girl's shaved head. "I can wait."

Love might be growing in the Valley, along with magenta flowers.

"So what exactly do people do at parties?" I ask.

Leia turns to me. "What do you mean?"

"I want to do what people do at parties. So, what is that?"

"They hang out. Listen to music. Dance. Drink." She grins at Baby Girl. "Hook up."

"What about weed?"

Leia shrugs. "Sometimes there's weed."

"My weed days are over," Baby Girl says. "I'm still clearing resin out of my head."

"Will there be weed tonight?" I ask.

"Maybe," Leia says.

"I want to smoke some weed," I say.

"I didn't think you were that kind of person."

The person I was isn't working. She never worked.

I say again, "I want to smoke some weed."

"First of all, smoking gives you lung cancer. And you know where I stand on that. Let's see if anyone has an edible."

"Great. Have you ever been high before?"

"Yes," Leia says matter-of-factly.

"What does it feel like?"

Baby Girl says, with a hint of nostalgia, "Like . . . you're in your body but not in your body."

"Fantastic. I want to get high."

Leia laughs. "Just whatever you do, stick to one edible."

"Why?"

"Just trust me."

I take two.

And when they kick in, it's like nothing I've ever felt before. My feet are on the ground, but my head is in the clouds, and I know what it feels like to be a bird. To walk and fly in one body. For all my life I've been chasing this feeling, and all I needed to do was get high. But instead I followed Chief's rules and his schedule and his stupid grocery list.

The music is loud inside. People are everywhere. Leia introduces me to the roller girls—Pre-Keri-Us and Helen Killer and Annie Maul and so many more whose names go in one ear and fly right out the other. And they have muscles and tattoos and piercings and hair colors that clash with their auras, and yet it all looks so perfect.

And there are people making out everywhere. In the bathroom. In the bedrooms. On the couch. Auras swirl together—tangerine mixing with eggplant mixing with midnight blue. It's a rainbow of bodies.

I can only half listen to what people are saying, because my skin keeps distracting me. It feels like I'm covered in a suit that I could take off and set to the side. I want to live in someone else's skin suit. Like Leia's. Then I would know what it's like to kick some ass and to love with reckless abandon.

I understand why Baby Girl tries on so many personalities. It feels good to set myself aside tonight and be someone new.

"Can we trade bodies?" I ask Leia. "I think mine is broken." I knock on my head. "I can't feel a thing."

She laughs. "That's the weed."

"Freud said, 'Everyone is broken. Get used to it, and always have a spare tire,'" Baby Girl says.

"No one here looks broken. They all look . . . badass." I grab Leia's bicep. It's like my hands have their own brains tonight. They're working without my consent. "I can't even do a push-up."

"You just need to practice," she says.

"Luca gave me roller skates," I confess. "He thinks I'm stronger than I am."

"Or maybe he sees something you don't." Leia shoves my arm, right where my muscles ache, and I wince.

"How is it possible to look in the mirror every day and not see myself correctly?" I ask.

"I've been wondering the same thing for eighteen years," Baby Girl says.

"It's because corporate America manipulates you to see what *they* want you to see so you buy their products," Leia adds. "Even though they're all stuffed with parabens that cause breast cancer. But as long as you smell 'powder fresh' and don't have white lines on your black shirt, your life is moving in the right direction and boys will like you."

"I haven't worn deodorant in years," Baby Girl says.

"You're better without it," Leia says.

"You're a freaking prophet," I say.

"I just don't like bullshit," Leia says.

"I'm pretty sure I painted bullshit on my sister's walls," I say.

"So paint over it," Leia says, like it's nothing.

"But I hid the paints in the basement, and now I'm afraid to go down there." I try to make a muscle, but my arm is Jell-O. "See, I'm a wimp."

And right then, Helen Killer breaks into our conversation. "No more talking! More dancing!" She grabs Leia and Baby Girl and me and drags us into the living room, where music is blasting and people are dancing and no one gives a shit how expensive the furniture is. People are standing on couches and jumping off tables, and I'm pretty sure a vase is smashed on the ground, but the music plays on.

Leia starts bouncing to the beat and swinging her arms, and soon her dark hair is flying all around her and she's laughing uncontrollably. She takes Baby Girl by the hands and pulls her close, and they give each other this look that says, *It's OK. Go a little crazy.*

So Baby Girl does. She catches the beat, her hands clasped with Leia's.
"Come on, Wren!" Pre-Keri-Us yells in my ear.

"I don't want to break anything."

"Don't worry about that! It isn't a party unless something breaks!"

Pre-Keri-Us howls like a wolf, and the rest of the roller girls echo her. It's loud and powerful. The room has gone completely wild.

And wild is catching.

It starts in my toes and travels up my legs and into my belly and out to my arms, and before I can contain it, before I can think any better, I'm howling, too. And dancing with every inch of me, like I've never done before. My hair sticks on my lips and tickles my nose, and I whip my head around, making the room blurry, and spin. But this is what I wanted tonight.

Then Leia is next to me, practically exploding. "Dance, Wren! Dance until you can't feel it anymore!"

And I know what she means—dance until my worries go numb. Until all I can feel is the burn in my muscles and the sweat on my skin. Until now I never understood why Lizzie spun herself into a tizzy. Why she would want the world to be in chaos.

Because in chaos it's impossible to focus. You can't overthink. You can't analyze. You can't even see straight. All a person can do is *be* and let the world spin around her.

I get it now.

Leia laughs, and Baby Girl smiles, and I jump until my legs hurt and my heart is pounding so hard I think it might come out of my chest. I look down and swear I can see it knocking, like a bird in a cage, trying to break free.

Knock, knock, who's there? Are you going to let me out?

When I look up, Baby Girl and Leia are kissing. But it's not like other people hooking up with desperate, hungry lips and hands. Baby Girl and Leia are slowly discovering each other, taking their time, right here in the world's messiest living room, and it's beautiful.

"Can I shave your head?" Leia shouts over the music.

Baby Girl says, "Only if you're careful with me."

Leia takes Baby Girl's hand in the gentlest of ways, in the same manner Lizzie held Baby Girl when she was sad and broken in junior high—preciously—and they disappear upstairs.

It's magical, and I want Luca to touch me like that. Tears spring to my eyes before I can hold them back, so I go outside and lie under a blanket of stars. The night smells like a forest floor, like pine needles and dirt, even in the suburbs, where people cut down too many trees and hate messes. I lie like a gigantic starfish, sinking into the earth and letting it hold me like a mother should.

I'm lying there by myself for what feels like a while. Each second that I'm here, I'm not with Luca. That fact sits heavy on my chest, making it hard to breathe. When the chaos settles, reality inevitably returns.

I take my phone from my pocket to text Wilder.

Me: I'm stoned

Wilder: I'm jealous

Me: I can't feel my legs

Me: Or my tongue

Wilder: Wicked

Me: Problem is I can still feel my heart

Wilder: That's the rub

Lying back on the grass, I let my heart beat as it wants—wild and chaotic and broken and whole at the same time. Because *that's* the rub—that something broken continues to work.

In the background the party hums and life moves, broken and messy. Time slips away. Second by second. Breath by breath. Somewhere love is wandering the streets of Spokane. Waiting. And I know what it feels like to wait. Love shouldn't have to.

Somewhere the sun is shining cadmium yellow in the night.

Lizzie is right. Monet hated lines, and yet I've painted too many of them.

Me: I think I want to start a revolution

Wilder: How?

Me: It's time to open the window Wilder

25

THE BUS STOP TO NOWHERE

Leia and Baby Girl drop me off at Happy Homes Assisted Living Center. It didn't take much to find Luca. All I had to do was text him. That's the rub—doing what's easy is sometimes the hardest of actions. Luca told me to meet him here.

It's late, well past my curfew. We had to drive around while I slugged down coffee, with all the windows down so the cool wind and caffeine could put my head back into place.

We eventually found the light in the dark. Luca sits at the bus stop in front of the assisted living center. An ellipsis forced to be still, waiting. I'm sorry I took so long.

"You need to start thinking of a name," Leia says as I climb out of the car. One of her hands grasps the steering wheel. The other holds Baby Girl's.

"A name?"

"Your Roller Derby name."

Baby Girl says, "Once you put a name to something, you can't go back. Choose wisely. Labels are hard to pull off cleanly."

"And some labels lie," Leia says. "Beware of deli meat." She looks at Baby Girl with admiration and intimacy. "You're a goddamn genius. You know that, right?"

"I wish I would have known that in high school. I would have gotten better grades."

"Most teenagers are so hopped up on synthetic sugar, high-fructose corn syrup, and food coloring, it's a wonder our brains work at all. And parents think weed is a problem. It's the most natural thing we put in our bodies."

"I love when you talk," Baby Girl says. "I have keys to the carousel downtown. You want to break in and take a ride with me?"

"I'd do anything with you."

As they leave, love hangs out the window of Leia's truck and waves goodbye.

I sit down next to Luca, not so close that our legs touch, but enough to flirt with the line of intimacy and warmth, and I don't waste a second soaking up his cadmium-yellow light. When you miss something that much, you hug it close when it comes back. Now isn't the time to play coy. Or play . . . anything.

Now is the time to exist.

For a while the only sound is the light summer wind traveling through the night, passing its way through Spokane to rattle the leaves and swirl loose garbage in parking lots.

"When does the bus come?" I ask.

"No one really knows."

"Well . . . where are you going?"

"I'm not sure yet," he says. "Alaska sounds kind of nice."

"That's a long trip. I'd miss you if you went to Alaska."

Luca looks at me. "You would?"

"I would." My leg inches over to touch his.

"OK. I won't go to Alaska. Vancouver?"

"Still too far." Now my shoulder touches his.

"Seattle."

"Not good enough." I place my hand on his leg.

Luca glances down at it. "I'm sorry. When you touch me, I lose all perception of time and place."

"We should probably just stay here, then." Taking Luca's hand in mine, I skim my palm against his and slowly tangle our fingers together.

"It's a good thing the bus never stops here," Luca says.

"Sounds like we'll be waiting here for a while. Why don't you tell me a story in the meantime?"

So Luca tells me what happened. About his grandma, how she lived with him ever since he was a baby. How she has calloused hands from living on a farm most of her life, how her hands match her personality, and how even though she is rough, he loves her fiercely.

And then last year she started forgetting things.

"She still knew how to can peaches, but she couldn't remember my brother's name."

"What about you?" I ask.

"She always remembers my name."

"That's because you're unforgettable." I smile.

"God, I missed my marshmallow."

And then he tells me about the night of our date. He left her home alone. His dad was working late, and his mom was at a book club.

"But I'm impatient. And I wanted what I wanted right then."

"What did you want?" I ask.

"You," he says.

So he left his grandma alone, thinking she would be OK. But when his dad got home from work, she was gone. His dad panicked. That's when Luca got the call.

"I was supposed to take care of her," he says. "I was selfish. I thought she'd be OK."

They eventually found her wandering downtown, looking for the bus that goes to Colfax, where her farm was. She was desperate to go home.

"But my family sold that farm fifteen years ago when my grandma came to live with us. It hasn't been her home in years. We're her home. Or . . . we *were* until a few days ago," Luca says. After she went missing, his dad decided then that they weren't capable of taking proper care of his grandma themselves, so they moved her to the assisted living center.

"It's my fault she's here now," Luca says. "I really fucked things up this time."

"Luca . . . ," I say. "This isn't your fault."

"It isn't?" he says sarcastically. "Whose fault is it? If I hadn't left her alone, she wouldn't have gone missing. I could have stopped her."

"But you can't stop her memories from fading," I say. "She's safer here."

"As safe as a person can be when their memories abandon them." He pauses, then adds, "It's the noise I can't get over. I'm used to her noise in the house. The way she shuffled her feet. It's not there anymore. When someone has been in your house for so long, when they're gone all of a sudden, it feels . . ."

"Empty," I say. I know the feeling.

He turns his beautiful brown eyes to mine.

"I can't leave her."

"That's why you stopped going to work and Driver's Ed."

"Let me tell you, I'm a damn good bingo player. I'm thinking of going professional. And the best part is, the competition just keeps dying off."

He's attempting to be funny, but truth has a way of etching itself on the canvas.

"I don't deserve freedom, Wren," Luca says. "Not when she's locked up here."

"I'm sorry," I say.

"Forget Alaska. Maybe the bus can take us back in time."

"I don't think that's possible. And I'm starting to think going back in time is overrated."

"You're probably right," Luca says.

"So I guess we still don't know where to go."

"Don't worry. This is all an illusion. They built this bus stop so people like my grandma have a place to sit when their memories come back and they want to run away. Everyone feels better when they *think* they're going somewhere. But the bus never comes."

"What happens when the bus never shows up?"

"By then no one remembers why they sat down in the first place."

My thumb skims Luca's hand.

"Now it's your turn to tell me a story," he says.

"I don't have any good stories."

"That's a lie."

"OK. It totally is. But where do I start?"

"Start where all good stories start," Luca says. "Once upon a time . . ."

I rest my head on his shoulder. It feels like coming home. Luca is my undoing and my becoming all at once.

"Once upon a time . . . ," I say, and start at the beginning, taking apart each piece of my life, unwinding the story bit by bit. I tell him about a mother who left, a father too sad to live in the sun, the forest growing in my own house, Lizzie and her postcards, the small make-believe lies that created a better life, Lizzie's leaving, the numbness, the vacancy.

I tell him how I went cold, frozen. How I sat in my room for days after she left, looking out the window, waiting for her to walk up the driveway. I couldn't eat. I couldn't sleep. I couldn't move. Chief would talk, but the sun was gone, and I was wilting.

I tell Luca how Chief finally picked me up, held me like a baby, and made me go to the doctor. And when the doctor asked what hurt, what was wrong, I told him, "My heart."

So they monitored and scanned, and my heart beat like it should. Doctors always lack imagination. My doctor saw only the organs that make a body, not the shattered story that made my eyes and hair and skin. The love between two parents that was scraped together one night in hopes that holding it close would make them a whole unit again. But my mom dissolved in Chief's arms until all that was left was a baby, not the woman he wanted.

"There's nothing wrong with you," the doctor said. "Your heart's fine."

"There's a bird in there," I said. "I can feel her flutter sometimes."

The doctor looked at me like I was crazy. "Are you trying to tell me that you swallowed a bird?"

The wings stopped moving. Suddenly I couldn't feel her.

"What happens when a bird stops flapping its wings?" I asked.

"It falls to the ground, I guess."

With eyes glazed over and limbs dead, I gazed through the window in the room. Rain fell on the glass and dribbled down in streaks.

"I better hold on tight to the wire, then."

I tell Luca how I used to paint for Lizzie, but how ever since she left, I couldn't seem to pick up a brush. How I couldn't see anything in life worth capturing and holding, until now.

I tell Luca my story until the scraps of the past are piled at my feet and I feel weightless.

This bus stop might really be magic.

Our hands are still linked, my eyes trained on our entwined fingers. If Luca's skin wasn't slightly darker than mine, I wouldn't know which finger belonged to who, the two of us blurring together.

"Lizzie just left?" he asks. "No note? Nothing?"

"I woke up and she was gone. Since then it's been nothing except the postcards."

He sits up. "That doesn't make any sense. Something must have happened."

"It does if you knew Lizzie. She was . . . untethered. Just like my mom. Even Chief knew it. It's like . . . he expected her to leave at some point, as hard as he tried to stop it. He knew, once she turned eighteen, it was only a matter of time. I think when she left, a part of him was relieved."

Luca turns to me in earnest. "Wren, Happy Homes built this bus stop for patients who are desperate to leave. But they always have a reason. It might not make sense to us, but it makes sense to them."

I thought *I* was the reason. When I found her room empty, the hammock still, I blamed the curse. On some level I thought I deserved it. I was needy for her love, wanting more, craving every morsel Lizzie could give me, and I thought Lizzie wanted to be relieved of that.

But I created a forest in her room so she could go wandering safely at night and search for the love she was missing. And she didn't have to look far. I was just across the hall. Lizzie knew how much I loved her. It was *I* who thought that it wasn't enough, that Lizzie always felt a sip below full and that I couldn't fill that space. Nor Baby Girl. Nor the trees and the moon and the flowers.

"But what's the reason?" I ask.

Luca places his warm hand on my cheek and says, "Wren, maybe she found your mom."

26

A KISS TO CONSUME

Luca has his phone out, too quickly. My heart can't handle the pounding in my chest. The high I felt earlier is distant, receding.

"What's her name?" he asks.

"Whose name?" It feels like there's cotton in my ears.

"Your mom's. I'll google her."

His fingers are typing, and the world is spinning, and I still can't believe what Luca just said. Did Lizzie find our mom? Is that why she left? Why wouldn't she tell me or bring me with her?

"Stop, please," I beg. "I don't want you to google her."

"Why not? This could be the missing piece."

It's not like Lizzie and I never thought of this. The idea of searching the internet for our mom has spent so much time in my head, it's built a home, brick by brick and room by room, in a corner of my brain. A home full of chairs and tables and dishes that make noise when they rattle and move, distracting me almost daily.

Why?

Because my mom left me. Because she thought I was untouchable. Simply putting her name in a search bar makes it all . . . real.

And then I might see her, and love her instantly, and break all over again. That's the shittiest part—love happens even when you don't want it to. Like breathing in and breathing out, it's an involuntary reflex. Love hits the veins, and within milliseconds it's everywhere. It's the most heartbreaking reality of being her child. I long for her love, whether she wants to give it or not. It's a thirst I will always have. But it's better to starve out the thirst than quench it with saltwater.

Lizzie and I knew searching for her would lead to more. Desperate people cling, grasp, claw, and yet all that work only leaves their fingernails bloody and torn. Our mom would still be gone, Lizzie and I the ones in pain.

The one time Lizzie went into that dark basement, and returned a little more shattered, was enough for me.

I take Luca's phone from his hands and set it on the bench.

"She didn't want me, Luca. Why should I want her?"

He cups my face with his hands. "This isn't about her. It's about Lizzie. Wren, this might be the answer we need."

Time stops. Even the wind pauses for this moment.

"We?"

"You can't think, after everything you told me, that I'm just going to walk away and let you deal with this on your own." Luca's thumb caresses my cheek lightly. Tears wet my skin. "I'm not letting you go through this alone. You're my marshmallow, Wren."

His lips come a little closer to mine.

"No one's ever wanted me before," I whisper.

"This goes beyond want," he says. "I'm consumed by you, Wren. Now, I think I've been patient enough. I'm going to kiss you."

"Are you sure you want to do that? My toes haven't changed."

"Thank God."

His mouth is on mine then. He pulls me closer, and I don't resist. I hold him to me, mesmerized. I've never kissed anyone before, never thought it possible for a person to want to taste what I'm made of. To want to hold each part of me—my bones, my flesh, my being—in his hands.

Each movement Luca makes—his lips parting, his mouth opening to mine, his hands tangling with my hair—sends waves of heat through my body, deeper than the skin, deeper than my organs, to the pit in my stomach. To the space I knew could never be occupied.

I was living dissolved, particles barely held together, as time and memory took pieces from me, until I thought I wasn't worth the space I occupied.

But now . . .

Luca pulls back momentarily to whisper my name against my lips. Off Luca's tongue, it sounds like a song—a calling home.

I'm so thankful for this bus stop to nowhere, where a bus will never come and take me out of this moment. Out of this life. Here, we can stay. Intertwined, where make-believe and reality intersect and love takes a seat, waiting for what's next as the worry of the past melts away.

Our lips separate, though our noses still touch, and Luca's thumb caresses my cheek.

"What's her name, Wren?" he asks again, warm breath flowing from his lips to mine, carrying strength in his words.

But I'm not ready. I don't want to leave this moment with Luca. I just found myself.

If Lizzie *did* find our mom, why leave me behind? Why leave in silence, in the black of night? There's more to this story—the dark kind of more—and I'm not sure I can handle that right now. I just found the sun again.

"Please just kiss me again."

And Luca does.

Morning on the Seine Near Giverny, 1897

Dear Songbird,

Did you know that Monet was so fed up with boring, formulaic art that he decided to chuck it all and end his life by jumping into the Seine, like a madman? But he survived. It was only after that that he started painting the way he wanted to.

I guess it was a good thing he went a little crazy. And lived to paint about it.

I love you,

Lizzie

Wren Plumley
20080 21st Ave.
Spokane, WA 99203

27

BABY STEPS

I stand in my room, Wilder in his, both of us framed by open windows. The cool night air flows in, and I can still feel Luca on my lips.

Wilder and I stare at each other, as if seeing the real us for the first time.

"You did it," I say directly to him. No phone needed now.

He takes a cautious breath, holding his hands on his chest, as if it might explode. But it doesn't. And when Wilder exhales, so do I.

"I did." His voice is soft and sweet.

But I can see the hesitation still lingering on his face. "What's wrong?" I ask.

"Only seventy percent of people wash their hands after using the bathroom."

"That's really gross, Wilder."

"I know. And bacteria double their number every twenty minutes. I've done the math. I don't suggest you do it. The numbers are staggering." He eyes the outside world skeptically. "Bacteria outnumber most life-forms on the planet."

"But without bacteria, the earth wouldn't have soil to grow plants," I offer.

"That's true." Wilder looks at me. "Baby steps."

"Baby steps," I repeat.

He leans his body halfway out of the window.

"There's life down there," he says, pointing to the earth one story below. "But that grass could have pesticides on it. Or a bug could crawl into your mouth and lay eggs in your stomach, and the next thing you know, you'll have a tapeworm." Wilder offers me a sad expression. "What if I get sick again, Wren? Now that I've felt fresh air, how can I ever go back inside and not miss it?"

I climb up onto the windowsill. "Baby steps," I say.

Wilder cautiously climbs up onto his windowsill, across from me, and we're both perched there, two people on a precipice, waiting to jump.

"There are between ten thousand and ten million bacteria on each hand," he says. "Damp hands are ten thousand times worse."

"One kiss can hold up to eighty million bacteria," I say.

"Kissing sounds lethal. I don't think I'll ever risk it."

"It's worth it."

Wilder glances toward the earth once again. "Life is down there."

"It's not all tapeworms, Wilder."

"Just be careful, Wren."

28

BRAND NEW

I'm grounded. Olga tells Chief that I was out past my curfew, and I despise her even more for paying attention.

Wheel of Fortune is on. It's Couples Week.

Chief is huffing and puffing like a dragon around the house. "What's my vegetable?"

He is having a hard time finding his words this morning. He's thinking more than talking, which is never a good sign.

"You're a carrot," I say.

Leia is broccoli. She has so many ideas sprouting out of one stalk.

Baby Girl is a tomato. She can't decide whether she's a fruit or a vegetable.

Chloe is a jalapeño. On the outside she looks innocent, but if you take a bite, fire eventually consumes you.

And Luca is a green bean—long and thin and tasty.

"We should eat green beans more often," I say out loud, dreamily. "I'll add them to the grocery list. I really do love green beans." And then I realize what I've said. "I mean, I *like* green beans. I couldn't possibly *love* green beans. It's been too short of a time for love."

I might still be a little high.

"Stop talking about vegetables, and tell me where you were last night," Chief says, beer in hand.

"With a friend," I say. *At a party. Where I got high. And then I kissed a boy. Numerous times.* "Do you want to know why you're a carrot?"

"No." He slugs his beer.

"You're skinny, firm, crisp, and grow in the dark."

"We're not talking about carrots right now."

"We should. You need to change your diet. You don't realize it, but it's killing you."

"No, *you're* killing me right now. What were you doing last night?"

"I told you. I was out with a friend."

"Who?" Chief asks firmly.

I don't want to tell Chief about Luca or Leia. He'll investigate. He'll do his cop thing. I don't want him interfering.

"Wilder."

"Who is Wilder?"

Lies trip off my tongue surprisingly fast. Chief can't know that Wilder is "what's going on" next door either. He'd march over there. And Wilder just got the courage to open the window. He doesn't need a cop banging on the door, yelling at him. "I met him at the library."

"And what were you doing with *Wilder*?"

"Stop interrogating me like I'm a criminal. We didn't do anything illegal." More lies. "So, what's my vegetable?"

"I want to meet this Wilder."

"You can't," I say quickly.

"And why not?"

"He's sick."

"What do you mean he's sick?"

"Tapeworm."

"What?"

"He's got a tapeworm. It's a pretty shitty situation." I try to smile. "Get it? Shitty?"

"Stop being cheeky, Wren."

I ease back. "Look, Chief, I'm sorry. I lost track of time. I won't do it again. But this is what you wanted, right? For me to have a life? You can be mad I was late, but you can't be mad I made a friend."

Lately he's been extra cop-ish, his mustache framing a perpetual frown. Like the night lingers in his bones, even during the day, and the sunshine through his window can't melt it as he sleeps.

Something is weighing on him, and it's more than just Lizzie being gone.

We both sit on the couch, Chief and his beer, me and my cereal. Pat Sajak and Vanna White give us word puzzles to solve.

"I was talking to your aunt," he finally says, "and apparently their local high school in Utah has a really great art program. The best in the state."

"That's good for Utah." *Apparently* Chief didn't understand that all discussions about Utah were over weeks ago. It's too dry in Utah. Deserts can't be trusted. They're too one-sided. I like that Washington can't decide whether it's rainy or sunny most seasons. I switch topics.

"Why don't you date?" I ask.

He spits out some of his beer. "Jesus Christ, Wren."

"You've never been on a date."

"I've been on plenty of dates."

"Not for the past eighteen years you haven't. That's quite a drought."

"I don't have time to date," he says. Chief suddenly looks extra chapped, like life was sucked out of him a long time ago. I'm just starting to notice how bad it really is.

And I can't stop touching my lips and thinking about how today feels better than any day I've lived before.

"Maybe you should make time," I say. "Maybe going on a date would help."

"Help with what?"

With the empty room in Chief's heart, and the clogged gutters that choke him in the middle of the night. Love might just be the water he needs.

"Hydration," I say.

"That doesn't make any sense."

"Most people don't drink enough water."

"I'm hydrated." Chief shifts uncomfortably in his seat and slugs a huge gulp of beer.

"Beer dehydrates you."

Chief groans and sets down the can. "Stop acting like the parent, Wren."

"But if I don't take care of you, who will?"

"I can take care of myself."

"That's a lonely existence," I say. "Believe me, I tried."

He gives me this look that speaks without speaking, and it says, *Back off.* But for my entire life, I've backed away.

"We never talk about her," I say. This is not googling my mom's name like Luca wants me to do, but it's a step.

"Who?" But Chief knows who I'm talking about. I eye him intently. "There's nothing to talk about. She left. We moved on. There's no need to look back. She sure didn't."

But Chief is actually stuck. He hasn't moved an inch. Just because we physically left Boise doesn't mean his heart came with him.

"Was she a pea?" I ask.

"What?"

"Since you're a carrot, was Mom a pea? Was she round and squishy and a little sweet? Did you go together like peas and carrots?"

Chief stands and frowns.

"You can categorize people all you want, Wren, but it's more complicated than that. *Life* is more complicated than that." He retreats upstairs, acting like the carrot that he is—stuck in the ground, covered in darkness. Before he disappears, he says, "I'm sorry to hear about your friend's tapeworm, but you're grounded for a week."

On Monday Luca sits next to me in Driver's Ed and pulls a peanut-butter-and-jelly sandwich from his bag. Sometimes when I'm with him, I feel like I could forget to breathe, and still I would survive.

"I'm grounded for breaking curfew," I say.

"Bummer." He sets half on my desk.

"It was worth it." My foot reaches for Luca's, and we meet in the middle with a simple touch. "I'm glad you came back to class. How's your grandma?"

"Same. How are your toes?"

"Same."

Luca wiggles his eyebrows at me. "Since we've already established that my patience is extremely lacking, do you mind if we just skip the awkward weeks of wondering if we're boyfriend and girlfriend and jump to the part where we are?"

My stomach jumps to my throat. "OK," I say. "And since we're skipping things, can we avoid the uncomfortable will-we-or-won't-we-kiss-again scene and you just kiss me?"

"You have a deal."

But when Luca's lips are about to touch mine, Mr. Angry Driver's Ed Teacher coughs. Startled, we separate and sit back in our desks.

The peanut-butter-and-jelly sandwich tastes bland compared to kissing.

The class begins, and Luca gets a piece of paper from his backpack. He writes:

You smell good

And I write:

It's the peanut butter

And he writes:

You have some on your cheek

I move to clean it up, but Luca stops me with his hand. He gently rubs my cheek, letting his thumb linger softly, his skin warm on mine.

He writes:

I lied—I just wanted to touch you

It's astounding how the simple act of acknowledgment can transform a life.

I write:

I think I have peanut butter on my fingers

Luca takes my hand in his and turns my palm upward, his fingertips inspecting the skin there, inch by inch. He does the same with the other hand. His light touch has my head spinning.

He writes:

Anywhere else?

I write:

My lips

Luca offers me this grin that sends my stomach on a ride and pulls my entire body tight with anticipation. His thumb comes to my bottom lip, skimming it and turning me inside out.

Then he writes:

You're quite the messy eater

And I think, *That's what happens when you're starved for attention your entire life.* That's what happens when the untouchable is finally touched. I want Luca everywhere.

Right here in Driver's Ed, surrounded by the ugliness life can offer—old carpet and asbestos and a paneled drop ceiling with water marks—among all the rundown sadness, two people sit next to each other, coaxing life to the surface.

When we leave, Luca says, "See you tomorrow," and I know what he means. He means, *Tomorrow, I will see you with my entire being. I will cover you again.*

It's like I've been baptized in Luca.

I'm born, brand new.

"See you tomorrow, Luca."

The next day, Wilder stands in his backyard, feet on the cement, his toes lined up with the grass.

"Should you really be outside, since you're grounded?" he asks.

"I think I was grounded for my entire life until a few weeks ago," I say.

"What about Olga? You don't want to get into any more trouble, Wren."

"She's watching a *Real Housewives of Atlanta* marathon." I pull a blade of grass from the ground. "I'm allowed to be outside. I just can't leave the property."

"What about the roof?"

I glance in the direction of the garage. "I don't know. I forgot to ask."

Wilder stands still, toes tickling the edge of the lawn.

"I don't think this is a good idea," he says.

"You won't know unless you try."

"There's safety in holding still. Not rocking the boat. I mean, look at you. You got in trouble. You're grounded. You shouldn't have broken curfew."

"It was worth it."

"Was it? To be locked up for a week?" Wilder gives me this pained look, like he's trying to hold on to something that's slipping away. "You're changing, Wren."

"What's wrong with that?"

"I'm just . . . worried," he says. "What if it all falls apart?"

"I did some research on tapeworms," I say. "And it turns out, they're not that hard to cure. Some people don't even know they have them. They cure themselves."

"What are you saying?"

"You don't need to be afraid of the grass, Wilder."

"I thought we were in this together, Wren."

"We are."

"It feels different now."

"Just step on the grass, Wilder."

"It's not the grass I'm worried about, Wren," he says. "It's you."

29

A MEMORY WORTH SUFFERING FOR

We're all together—Leia, Baby Girl, Luca, and me. Leia and Luca are on a work break. He hasn't missed a shift since the night we kissed.

The day is hot, the August summer sun clouded only by light smoke in the air from wildfires in Canada. Some days in the summer, the air quality can get so bad, Chief doesn't like me going outside. But soon enough September will knock on August's door, bringing clouds and rain and the foreshadowing of October's wind.

Today the pavement sizzles underneath us as Leia and I roller-skate in the parking lot behind Rosario's Market. Luca rides his skateboard, almost frenzied, as if trying to exert as much energy as he can before going back inside. Baby Girl seems content to watch Leia.

"You need to start a workout regimen," Leia says to me. "And no more shitty food."

"I'm done with shit," I say. I threw out the grocery list. I can no longer be an accomplice to Chief's slow destruction by synthetic sugars and Yellow Number Six. I know better now, and I love him too much.

"Push-ups, crunches, lunges, tricep dips, squats," Leia says. "Ten to twenty reps a day."

"I'm happy to coach you," Luca says as he skims by on his board, the rush of wind from his body landing squarely on mine. "To make sure you're doing the squats right, of course." He offers a passing wink that sends my stomach flipping.

Leia shows me the toe-stop drills I need to practice, and how to do a crossover.

"Step-ups," she adds, demonstrating on the picnic table where Baby Girl sits in the shade, watching. "You need to strengthen your left leg."

By the time we're done, I've fallen six times, have a scrape on my elbow that's bleeding down my arm, and am drenched with sweat. My legs might crumble, but the pain is beyond good. I crave it now.

"How about Strawberry Jam," Leia offers as we sit down next to Baby Girl.

"But I don't have red hair." Sweat rolls down my back.

"Miss Fortune," Baby Girl says.

Leia smiles at her. "I like that one."

"That sounds like a rich girl's name," I say.

"Lord of the Rink?" Leia suggests.

"Too nerdy," I say. "I'm not cool enough for that."

Luca rides at us like he's on water. He skids to a stop and pops his skateboard off the concrete. "Hot Brod. That's my vote. Get it, because you're a hot broad."

"Yes, Captain Obvious. We get it." Leia rolls her eyes. "Don't stress about a name, Wren. It'll come to you. Just work on drills for now." She checks the time on her phone. "Break time's over. Time to get back to the world of pesticides and BPA."

"But it pays the bills, Princess," Luca says.

"True," Leia says. "But if only we just left everything alone. Let an apple be an apple."

"A dandelion is a dandelion is a dandelion," Baby Girl says.

"I love how your mind works." Leia skims her hand over the crown of Baby Girl's head. "But people don't like seeing bruises. Even though we all have them. An apple isn't damaged just because of one little bruise."

"I hope not," Baby Girl says, so quietly that I'm not sure she meant for us to hear. She stands and stretches. "I'm due at the carousel."

"Save me a horse." Leia winks. "I'll come down for a ride later."

After Baby Girl and Leia have left, Luca sits down next to me.

"I'm not sure I can get my legs to move just yet," I say, taking my roller skates off.

He wipes a little spot of blood from my elbow. "You need a Band-Aid." Luca gets up and leaves, then reemerges from Rosario's Market with a first-aid kit. He wipes my elbow with an antiseptic wipe, cleaning the blood and blowing the skin dry. "It's not too bad."

Luca places the bandage carefully on my elbow.

"Almost done," he says. He leans down and places a kiss directly on top of the bandage. "All better now?"

"I think so." I'm floating. No more pain.

"That was my mom's trick when we were little, to get us to stop crying. A kiss to take the pain away."

"I don't think my mom ever did that for me," I say. "Not that I remember, at least."

"You don't remember her at all?" he asks.

"No."

"Maybe it's for the best."

Luca tells me that some days his grandma remembers everything. Other days she can't recall people's names. He can't decipher what really exists to her and what doesn't. Some days she hallucinates. It happens with dementia patients. People think they see things at night—bugs in their beds, spirits clinging to the walls, someone in the shadows waiting for them. At times she's convinced that the nurses at Happy Homes Assisted Living Center are stealing from her.

"Last week she told me a story from when I was little, and my dad said everything she said was true." Luca runs his fingertips over the bandage on my elbow. "Then the next day I go in to see her and she tells me she's been talking to my grandpa, who's been dead for fifteen years. The second I think she's back to being herself, she's gone. I never know what to believe."

"I'm sorry."

"I'm coming to terms with the fact that it doesn't really matter at this point," he says. "She won't remember her life, but she also won't know to miss it. It's us with the memories who suffer. So maybe you're better off not knowing your mom."

And yet . . . not knowing carries a burden, too. Which is worse?

Luca looks at me so intensely that my cheeks can't help but flush, and my stomach pulls tight.

"I can tell you one thing that *is* for certain: I don't ever want to forget you, Wren." He brings his hand to the bottom of my chin, his thumb lightly caressing my lip. "You're a memory worth suffering for."

He kisses me, as if to etch the moment so deeply into our minds that no one could erase it. As if to set a groove so deep it will leave a lasting impression, an indelible mark even time can't obliterate.

Right now, in this moment, it feels possible to hold on to something as elusive as a memory. To pin it down and set it in history as infinite. Never to be lost, forever to be believed.

"You are, too, Luca," I say. "You are, too."

30

BEFORE AND AFTER

"Before and After." Beer in hand, Chief says the *Wheel of Fortune* category from the couch. Pat Sajak looks extra orange, his clashing pickle-green aura making it hard to look at the television. I'm doing the daily exercises Leia assigned me. Chief eyes me as I count out squats. My quads, which until recently I didn't even know I had, are burning.

"First you come home with a wagon full of vegetables. Now you're working out? What the hell is going on, Wren?"

"I'm saving your life," I say.

"Wren, we discussed this. I don't need you to save my life. I'm fine."

But Chief was the one who told me why cops restrain people. "Most of the time, people need saving from themselves," he said once. "That's what the handcuffs are for."

"You don't want to grow man-boobs, do you?" I ask.

"What does that have to do with anything?"

"Do you know how much estrogen is pumped into cows?"

"Where is this coming from?"

I switch to push-ups. "The better question is, Why did it take me so long to figure it out?"

Chief shifts uncomfortably and focuses on Pat Sajak.

"Before and After." Chief points at the TV.

The contestant buys an *O.*

I'm mid-push-up when I say, "Hole in the *Wall Street Journal.*"

"Damn it. I should have gotten that." He retreats for another beer.

I start on lunges. "What's Mom's maiden name?"

"What?" Chief's voice sounds strained from the other room.

"Her maiden name. I don't know it."

There's a pause before he walks back into the room, cracking open a fresh beer. "Rhine. Why do you ask?"

"Just wondering." I switch the leg I'm lunging. "Did she change her name when you got married?"

"What's with all the questions this morning?"

"I don't know."

"No. She didn't change her name." He gives me the answer like it hurts to say it.

"Was she a feminist? Is that why?"

"Why does it matter?"

"I just want to know."

"Curiosity killed the cat, Wren."

"Cats eat birds," I say. "I like curiosity. We're on the same team."

Chief takes a swig of his beer and gives me a sideways glance. "You know what I mean. You've never been curious before."

"Things change," I say. I used to think a painted forest was all I needed, but it turns out the smell of real pine needles is better, even if the needles leave a sticky residue on your fingers.

"Clearly." Chief eyes me suspiciously.

"Was it love at first sight with Mom?"

He sinks a little deeper into the couch. "It was lust at first sight," he finally says, and brings his beer to his lips.

"What's the difference?"

"Lust is selfish. You have to be careful with it, Wren. It can be dangerous."

"What do you mean?"

"When you want someone that badly, it can make you blind to reality," he says. "Just trust me."

Even with his eyes on the television, I know Chief isn't watching *Wheel of Fortune*. He's replaying the past in his mind.

"Did you love her?"

"Yes," he states. "But love is a lot of work."

"Did you work at it?" I ask more emphatically.

"Every damn day."

"If that's the case, why did you let her go?"

My question seems to snap him out of his trance. "It's not that simple."

"But you loved her. You wanted to be with her. Why did you let her leave? Why not chase her down? Force her to come home?"

I know that love and I have just gotten acquainted, but I would chase after Luca until my feet started to bleed and my toenails fell off.

Chief stands, his mood shifting. "I said it's not that simple, Wren."

"Then explain it to me."

"You wouldn't understand."

That's been his excuse. Chief refused to talk to me and Lizzie about his relationship with our mom, claiming we weren't old enough to understand, as if he could protect us from pain, but pain moved into our house the moment Lizzie moved out.

I don't think Chief can talk about love without seeing it outlined in pain.

"Just try," I say. "I want to know."

"You don't want to know!" he yells. His voice startles me. "Wren, do you know why the world needs police?"

I don't respond.

"So they can turn themselves away from crime and let someone else clean up the mess. Let me do my job. I'll deal with the chaos of your mom so you don't have to carry the burden. That's what I did before she left, and that's what I continue to do after."

Chief goes up to bed before he's drunk his usual six beers.

A woman named Samantha makes it to the bonus round. Time expires before she's able to solve the puzzle, and she misses out on winning a new car.

31

WHEN THE LIGHTS GO OUT

It's the last day of Driver's Ed. Engines rumble in the background as Mr. Angry Driver's Ed Teacher tells us the mechanics of the go-cart and his expectations for the day. The course is set up as a simulation of real life, with stop lights, turns, some sections of the track that symbolize highway, others that indicate pedestrian roadway.

"This isn't a game," he says, his eyes dancing over Luca briefly. Luca is so excited he's practically bouncing. His yellow light is extra bright. I could bathe in it to warm myself, and it only makes me want him even more. "Follow the rules. If everyone passes the simulation, you'll have the rest of the time for some fun."

"I like fun," Luca says to me. "Do you like fun?"

"What's fun?" His pinky finger slyly knots with mine. "Fun is my middle name," I say.

"How radical of your parents. My middle name is just Jonathan."

"Actually, my middle name is Margaret. It's, like, the middlest of middle names."

For a moment I consider telling Luca about Chief's outburst, how he left his beer on the table, half-drunk, dripping with condensation that left a ring stain on the wood. He's holding something in or shutting something out. But why? My mom is gone. She has been for years.

"Are you OK?" Luca's question has a concerned edge to it.

"I'm nervous about the go-carts," I lie.

"What's there to be nervous about?"

"Chief always says that cars are weapons. They kill more people than guns."

Luca leans in close, his lips gracing the soft spot right at the base of my ear. "Don't worry. If anything happens, I'm here to give you mouth to mouth anytime you need it."

It takes every ounce of willpower to move away from him when Mr. Angry Driver's Ed Teacher clears his throat in our direction.

We pick two go-carts parked next to each other. I walk Luca through the proper safety steps.

"You want to check your mirrors," I say.

"There are no mirrors."

"Remember your blind spots."

"Baby Girl would say, 'Life is one giant blind spot.'" Luca revs his engine and smiles. "We see only what we want to see."

I put on my helmet. Is that true? It sure feels like that sometimes. That perspective taints our vision. What might I be missing with my own eyes?

The simulation starts, and Luca breaks all the rules instantly, forgetting about stop signs and never using his blinker. He is chaos personified. I hear the rumbling of engines and Chief's voice saying over and over again, *Guns have safety buttons. Cars have seat belts. Both are important.*

The memory of his strained voice and pained face replay in my head as I drive. Why is he holding on to the past so tightly? Is that what love makes you do?

By the time the simulation is over, my hands ache from gripping the steering wheel so tightly.

But the breeze feels good today against the blistering sun and dry heat.

We pull back into the starting area. I take my helmet off to air out my sweaty head.

"Now we can have some real fun," Luca says, revving his engine again.

"What would you call that?" I ask, wiping my forehead.

"Foreplay." He winks. "Catch me if you can, Hot Brod!" Luca takes off. My chest pinches with an instantaneous ache. The farther he gets from me, the worse it feels. I need him like I need the wind to blow. I press the gas pedal to the floor, and the go-cart lurches forward.

My hands grip the steering wheel. Luca takes a turn at a speed that feels unnatural. When I attempt the same thing, my cart rises onto just two wheels, but, ignoring the danger, I grip the steering wheel harder and press the gas.

But with every turn, I seem to lose ground. Luca just gets farther and farther away until he feels unattainable. Untouchable. I want to yell at him to slow down, but my voice won't reach him. It's like he's trying to leave me.

Chief's words echo in my head. *When you want someone that badly, it can make a person blind to reality.*

Am I being blind with Luca? Does he *really* want me like I want him? Or is this all going to end in disaster? Where's the proof that love *ever* works out? I've never seen it. Come the fall he'll go back to school without me. He'll be busy with a different life. He'll forget me. And I'll be left missing him. Wishing we could be together and knowing he's out of reach.

And then it happens. The moment is so quick, and yet I'm slow to process it.

Wilder is standing on the edge of the track, watching me.

"I told you it would fall apart, Wren. I warned you."

But when I look back, he's gone. Disappeared.

My vision goes blurry in the sunlight. Luca is so far away from me, I'll never catch him. A bead of sweat drips down my forehead. When I wipe at it, I realize I've made a mistake.

The collision comes from behind, jarring me. My head whips forward. My seat belt tugs against my chest like a vise grip, holding me back and crushing me. My forehead knocks so hard on the steering wheel that stars pop in my eyes.

I forgot to put on my helmet.

I've been careless.

Everything slows.

The lights go out. The world goes black. And shadows begin to whisper in the darkness.

Songbird, look at the moon, Lizzie says, her voice that of a child. She thumbs the scar on her leg from when she fell down the stairs. The moon hangs full, like it's taking up the entire night. *On nights like this, I can feel her. She's out there somewhere, calling to us. Can't you hear her?*

Our mom feels as tangible to me as the wind. She pushes and pulls, but when I try to grab her, nothing fills my hand.

That's just make-believe, Lizzie. It isn't real.

You know as well as I do, Songbird. Life is just one big made-up story. No one tells it the same.

Then what are we to believe?

Lizzie doesn't answer me.

And somewhere in the distance, I hear a woman crying.

32

THE RELIABLE SOURCE

Whiplash and a concussion—that's the doctor's diagnosis. The crash caused a pileup—a chain reaction of crash after crash after crash, but I was the only one without a helmet. Everyone else came out unscathed.

When he arrived at the track, half-asleep and looking worn down, Chief threatened to sue the driving company. I told him over and over again that it was my fault. That I forgot the helmet. That I was driving recklessly.

"How many times have I told you?" Chief said, his voice straining to remain calm. "Cars are weapons and should be treated as such."

I got all woozy and almost fainted right there, and Chief backed off. By the time we got to the hospital, he had calmed down.

Now he's filling out paperwork in the hallway, drinking coffee as I talk to the doctor. It's the same doctor who saw me two months ago, when Lizzie left and I went dark.

The pain in my head won't ease. The cold that I felt in my memory seems to settle in the marrow of my bones, and I can't get warm. So many things are swarming through my mind.

Wilder. Luca. Lizzie. I don't know what to believe. What's real?

She's out there somewhere, calling to us. Can't you hear her? Lizzie's voice echoes in my head.

"I remember you," the doctor says, flashing a light in my eyes.

"I remember you, too."

"Questionable heart problem and ingestion of a bird, I believe it was." He feels the base of my skull and the tender spot on my forehead before getting out a prescription pad and writing.

"You're drinking enough water?" he asks.

"Yes."

"Getting enough exercise?"

"Yes."

He hands me a prescription. "You have a mild concussion and slight whiplash. Take this prescription, ibuprofen for the headache and muscle pain, and rest. No strenuous activity for a week."

"A week? But I have Roller Derby training."

"One week won't kill you." He examines me again. "You look good, Wren. Much healthier."

"Thanks." But there's disappointment in my voice. When he turns to leave, I stop him. "My friend's grandma has dementia."

"I'm sorry to hear that."

"Some days she's fine, and then the next she's gone again."

The doctor sits down on the end of my bed. "The mind is a mysterious organ. And can be a frustrating one."

I don't know why I'm telling him all of this. There are so many puzzle pieces shifting around in my head.

"The brain is . . . peculiar," he says. "It's subjective at times."

"What do you mean?"

"It chooses when to remember and when to forget," he says. "And sometimes it simply believes what it wants to believe."

I know this well. But it still doesn't help me.

"So even the mind can't be trusted?"

The doctor pauses. "I've always found it best to ask the heart the hard questions. It's a more reliable source."

Chief walks in then. "Is she going to be OK?"

"Mild concussion," the doctor says. "But she'll survive."

"That's good to hear."

"Take care of yourself, Wren." With a soft touch on my shoulder, the doctor leaves.

Chief helps me off the bed, wrapping his arm around my waist tightly to hold me up.

"I'm OK, Chief," I say. "I can walk just fine."

"You scared the shit out of me today. Just appease your old man."

So I do. He hoists me into his arms easily, and I wonder how many times a night he has to do this, how many desperate people Chief has carried because they believed they weren't strong enough to survive on their own. Drug addicts. Domestic abuse. Suicide. He's seen it all. Carried so many bodies.

How many times has Chief taken on the burden for people when they couldn't hold themselves?

This isn't the first time he's done it for me.

I let him practically carry me to the car.

"Is it hard, Chief?"

"Is what hard?"

"Carrying people all the time."

"Only when they fight me," he says. "Some people just don't want to be carried."

"That's what happened with Lizzie," I say matter-of-factly, and then yawn. Outside, the sunlight intensifies the pain behind my eyes.

"Let's not talk about this right now," Chief says.

He opens the car door and sets me inside.

"Do you ever just want to let go?" I ask him.

"With you, Wren, *never*."

33

A BIRD COMES TO CALL

My room is all white. White walls. White comforter. The wooden floors creak and pop in the summer when they swell. In the winter I'd pretend I was covered in an avalanche, surrounded by cold white everywhere, hunkering down to stay warm. Lizzie's room was my canvas. I never bothered to paint mine because I thought it was useless. I had no color. Every time I looked in the mirror and couldn't see an aura, I knew it was pointless. I could paint my walls a rainbow, and it still wouldn't make me shine.

It was more important that Lizzie got what she needed. That Lizzie have a colorful landscape to wander and wonder in. When the endless nothingness of white got to me in the winter, I just crept down the hall to Lizzie's room and stood in the ever-growing summer forest for a while, waiting until I was warm again.

"I realized something, Songbird," Lizzie said one time. Snow was falling on the slushy roads, and the trees outside were leafless and brown, but in Lizzie's room it was perpetual summer. "You're the only bird in my forest. Are you lonely? Do you need another bird to play with?"

"No," I said quickly. I didn't want to compete with anyone for Lizzie's attention.

"Just tell me if you change your mind."

I said I would, even though I knew it would never happen.

"Lizzie," I asked, "do you think this forest really exists somewhere in the world?"

"Of course, it does, Songbird," she said.

"Where?"

"Right here."

"Then we never have to leave, do we?" I asked.

"That's up to you."

Nothing has changed in Lizzie's forest since I painted the first trees. They haven't gotten any taller. The flowers never wilt. The butterflies never head south for the winter, because it's *never* winter. It's an endless summer nightscape.

But I know now that it's a distraction, an illusion, a magic trick of the eye. I thought if I just kept adding to our encapsulated, motionless world, she wouldn't notice how fake it all was. We could live in the warmth, even on cold days.

But I wasn't fooling only Lizzie. I was tricking myself. And now that world is crumbling. Crumbling to reveal what's real. Even now, as Wilder and I sit in my backyard, I prefer the tickle of grass. The carpet in Lizzie's room only itches my skin now.

"You shouldn't have been there, Wilder."

"I was just trying to protect you," he says. "I'm worried. You're never home. You don't rely on me. What happens when you don't need me anymore?"

"I don't know."

"Maybe we should go back to the way it was. It was . . . safer."

I thumb the grass, letting each blade skim my skin. Even it pales in comparison to Luca's touch.

"We can't go back."

"Are you really sure that boy likes you? The moment things get hard for him, he runs. You know this. What's to say he isn't going to do that to you?"

Shaded by night, Wilder looks partially dissolved, not completely solid.

"You're right," I say. "I don't know what's going to happen. I don't even know what to believe."

"Doesn't that scare you?"

"I'm terrified."

"See? My point exactly. Save yourself the pain, Wren. End it now."

"I don't think I can."

"Why? We'll go back to the way it was—just the two of us. You can believe in me."

I close my eyes and try to listen to my heart.

"I don't think I want to do that, Wilder."

He goes silent.

"Nothing lasts," I finally say. "Not this. Not summer. The birds eventually leave for the winter. But if we wait it out . . ."

Off in the distance, I hear a song, whistled into the darkness.

And I whisper to the night, "The birds will come back."

Chief takes work off for two days to keep an eye on me. Luca texts me repeatedly, but I don't respond. The story isn't clear yet. My head hurts too much to think about it.

By the third day I can tell the sunlight is getting to Chief. He wasn't expecting this change in schedule. Nothing is going as planned this summer, and Chief is getting antsier and edgier with each unpredicted turn. Lines in his face that weren't deep two months ago are starting to show more.

The night covers him well. Chief can hide in the darkness, just how he likes it. Never fully seen. But daylight's nature is to expose.

Chief is relieved when he finally goes back to work, and Olga returns to her usual spot on the couch.

I'm lying in bed when Olga knocks on my bedroom door. She doesn't wait for me to answer before bringing a tray of food in. The moment is oddly maternal and unexpected.

"You need good food." She sets down a tray with homemade chicken noodle soup. "Good food heals the body."

"You cook?"

"I cook."

I've known Olga for fourteen years and can't remember a single time she cooked for us. "How did I not know that?"

"You never ask, so I never tell you."

I take a bite of the soup and wonder what else Olga hasn't told me simply because I didn't ask the right questions.

She looks around at my white room and shivers. "It's cold in here."

"It's always cold," I say. "Even in the summer."

"More reason to eat soup."

I take a bite.

"This is really good. Thank you."

"You rest now." Olga moves toward the door.

"Olga?" She turns and looks at me. "If good food heals the body, what heals the heart?"

"The truth," she says. "It might break it a little more at first, but a clean break eventually heals completely."

"And you know this from experience?"

"No one avoids heartbreak." She gives me a knowing look.

"Do you miss Lizzie, too?"

Olga smiles genuinely. "You know me—I like drama. This house has been too quiet lately. I want the noise back."

With that, she leaves.

Later that night I stand in Lizzie's doorway, staring at the walls, and all I see are the places I messed up painting the forest. The inaccuracy of the butterflies. The drips of dried paint along the floorboards.

This forest is no replacement for a real one. One that smells of grass and dirt. One where late-night mist settles near the ground, making everything cool and damp. One where leaves rattle in the breeze in the summer and change colors in the fall and die in the winter, only to bud again in spring.

My phone buzzes in my pocket.

Luca: Look outside ur window

I head back to my room, look out the window, and see him standing in the driveway. A rush of pure happiness, edged sharply with guilt, washes over me. I'm ashamed I've avoided him. And yet here Luca stands.

Luca: Hey

Me: Hey

Luca: You haven't texted me back

Me: I know

Luca: Is it because I smell bad?

Me: Nah

Luca: Am I a bad kisser?

Me: No

Luca: I know

Luca: It's the nose ring

Me: I love ur nose ring

Luca: Then what?

What if I'm imagining all of this? Convincing myself that Luca needs me? What if Chief is right, that lust has made me blind? And I don't know how the story ends. That scares me. I feel completely uncovered with Luca, vulnerable. Only a crazy person would expose herself to that. But maybe that's the point. That's what I want to type, but I can't find the courage to. Luca texts again.

Luca: Mkay I'll go

He starts to leave.
"Don't go!"
The truth is, I've missed him every second of every day since the last time I saw him. And that feels worse than vulnerability.
Luca smiles and presses his finger to his lips. He holds up his phone and texts again.

Luca: Does that mean I'm allowed inside??

I tiptoe downstairs as quickly as possible. Luca comes in the back door while Olga sleeps in the living room, snoring on the couch, though I wonder if she's faking it. Has Olga been awake this entire time, secretly standing watch when I thought she didn't care?
If she is awake, she doesn't stop me from taking Luca upstairs.
"How's your head?" he asks once we're inside my room and the door is closed. He moves to touch me, but I back away. A surge of visible pain flares in Luca's eyes. "What's going on, Wren? Did I do something wrong?"
"No," I say quickly.

"Then what is it?"

Wilder's window seems to scream at me. The light is off, but his words of caution echo loudly in my head. And yet . . . the doctor told me how fickle the mind is. It can't always be trusted. But some days it's hard to fight against it.

I close my eyes and feel the beat of my heart.

"I think I'm in love with you."

Luca's exhale is audible. "I can see why this might be a problem."

"You can?" I open my eyes.

"Yes." He is smiling. "But you don't have to worry. It's not a problem for us."

He takes my face in his hands, the nearness of him like a heat wave I was desperately longing for. "Because I am in love with you, too, Wren Plumley."

"You are?"

"I am." He says it as if he's uttering a fact. The sky is blue. The grass is green. One plus one equals two. Luca loves me. I *know* it's true.

"Will you stop avoiding me now?"

"I'm sorry."

"Don't be. I run from everything, remember? But I'm not doing that anymore. And I'm not going to do that to you. Do you believe me?"

And I know in my heart, I do. "Yes."

Everything feels better with him here—my head, my heart. My white walls seem to brighten and melt, as if I could run my hand along the paint and feel warm water. It feels humid and warm in my bedroom for the first time ever.

Luca sits down on the bed. I do the same, inviting the electricity of nearness to wrap around us. More heat. More melting. Puddles begin to form on my wooden floors.

"So . . . I've never been in a girl's room before. It's very . . . white in here. Not that I know anything about it. The only rule at my house was 'Don't break down any door or knock over any walls.' And you know how good I am at following the rules. My bedroom hasn't had a door in five years." Luca scans the room again. "I'm a little afraid to touch anything."

I scoot closer to him. "Don't be."

And he smiles. "Is that an invitation to get this room a little dirty?"

That's what my room needs. Dirt so something can grow. A place to plant a life. A real life. With trees that don't just climb the walls and stop where I choose but that reach their branches out the window, beyond our house, grabbing for more.

I'm done questioning and worrying. Nothing can grow out of anxiety except more anxiety.

"Don't move," I say. "I'll be right back."

I peel myself from him and go down to the basement, where I put all my paint supplies the day after Lizzie left. Easels and brushes and container after container of paint are stacked at the bottom of the stairs, untouched for months. I couldn't even look at them.

Luca hasn't moved. When he sees my load, he helps, setting all the paint and supplies on the floor.

"What should we do now?" Luca asks.

I open a tube of tangerine paint—a color I used to make Lizzie's butterflies—and squeeze some onto the tip of my finger, letting it run down my skin like hot wax before falling to the floor. Luca and I both watch the orange settle on the wood. The first speck of color in a white room. But it's not enough.

"We paint," I say.

My tangerine-covered finger smooths the surface of Luca's warm cheek, leaving a streak of color on his flesh. A devious grin pulls at his face, and I think, *This paint brings life.*

"This could get dangerous," he says.

I put a streak of lapis, the color of the twilight sky in Lizzie's frozen forest, on his other cheek.

"It's about time," I say.

It starts with a simple line of green. Luca's hand leaves a gentle stroke across a white wall that travels toward the floor, leaving a drip on the floorboard. Sometimes that's all it takes—one person to walk into the nothing and leave his mark. A mark of love. And my room grows from there.

Silently color exhales all around us. Not just on the walls, but on the floor and my bed. No place is off limits. No pattern to follow. Just unabashed being. Now.

Luca and I work slowly at first, quietly, so no one can hear. But once more color coats the walls, it becomes addicting, insatiable. As the world sleeps, we come alive in my tiny room. And I can't stop.

I swirl and spin, letting my brush find the walls and the floor and the air, with no care as to where it all lands. Paint dangles from my hair, my fingers, my nose. I shake everything off, not caring where it goes, wishing I could scream, and yet unwilling to threaten the moment. I don't want it to end. Luca watches me as I shatter and color spreads all over my white room.

And then it's his turn.

All the heartache. Of losing his grandma slowly, teasingly, inch by bloody inch. Of fear. Of running away when life gets hard. Of skipping the hard parts and only coasting through life. It all pours out of him.

In a life where control seems fruitless—where people's memories turn on them and leave, where love can be cast into darkness at the mind's request—to paint a blank canvas is to rage against the loss of it all.

Luca is wild, and it's beautiful. Tangible. I could touch him right now, and it would be as if his soul was in my hands.

When the walls drip with paint, the white barely visible, I turn my gaze toward my ceiling. I swear I feel cool water dripping on my cheek, the last of the avalanche's snow starting to melt.

I climb onto my bed, paintbrush in hand, and jump, swiping a slash of cadmium yellow across the ceiling. My brush is a knife, and the ceiling bursts open, air flooding in, the night stars coming to watch the color show.

Luca jumps on the bed, too. With each slash of color, more of the ceiling withers away until not a drop of water can be felt, only open sky. It's like breathing for the first time after crawling and digging out of the avalanche.

The excitement has me so distracted, it takes a while to realize my head is pounding. My body is exhausted.

I crouch down on my bed, the pain becoming too much.

Luca stops immediately. "Are you OK?"

"No strenuous activity," I say, heaving. "I forgot."

"Lie down." Luca edges me back on my bed, splattered paint everywhere, and brings a pillow behind my head. "Just close your eyes for a second."

My room hums. Luca's fingers run over my forehead and into my hair, gently stroking my scalp.

"Does this feel OK?" he asks.

The pain eases. He's pure magic. I nod slowly. Luca settles next to me.

"Luca," I whisper. I look into his warm brown eyes. Eyes the color of earth. "I want to exist with you, before it's too late."

And so I kiss him. There is no more waiting. He's next to me now, and tomorrow he might not be. Because happiness doesn't last, and memories fade, and seasons change, and a forest that never dies isn't ever truly alive to begin with.

I kiss him until the walls melt around us, until heat fills the cold room, until a bird that lived so long in painted trees flies away.

I roll on top of Luca, needing to feel him completely underneath me.

"Wren," he whispers, our mouths still touching. "Your head."

"It's fine," I say. "Better than fine."

Luca tucks my hair behind my ears. "Are you sure? I don't want to hurt you."

I answer with a kiss that dissolves into more, into not only my lips doing the exploration, but my hands and my hips. If Luca needs me to convince him, I will. With everything that I am, I'll give us a memory to hold on to.

This is real. This is what I want. I'm not afraid anymore. I'm strong.

Soon our clothes are scattered all over the floor, covered in paint, but Luca and I are focused on covering each other now. His lips travel to my neck, my ears, my collarbone. My bare chest breathes with his. Skin to skin. Life to life.

And as Luca and I create something new together, trees begin to sprout in my room, flowers burst from the floorboards, petals unfurl into brilliant colors, butterflies float through the air. Grass softens the surface beneath us. The sun warms everything from skin to sky. And the forest grows and grows and grows, with more light, more color, more warmth than I've ever experienced before. Vines tangle around us, holding us close, pressing every inch of us into one. Lips, hips, limbs. Everything is moving. Everything is breathing. Everything is alive.

And for the first time in my life, I hear a bird come through my open window, soaring, floating, flying, singing a sweet, friendly song that catches on the wind. I can hear it, if only in my heart. And I know I'm finally home.

Woman with a Parasol—Madame Monet and Her Son, 1875

Dear Songbird,

I know you've told me before that Monet is a genius, but now I get it. Sometimes, we're too close to a situation to really see it. Up close, all we notice are individual brushstrokes. But once we back up, the entire painting becomes clear. We can see how the artist methodically placed each stroke of color to build a story.

It's time to take a step back and look at the picture.

I love you,

Lizzie

Wren Plumley
20080 21st Ave.
Spokane, WA 99203

34

THE DIRTY PAST

A whisper is worse than shouting. Words softly spoken hang in the air, unlike words screamed, their impact felt but fleeting.

Lizzie left on a whisper. Hushed words barely audible, lost in the night. Surface pain wants to be loud. It throbs. It screams. Like a child who wants attention. Like a small paper cut that hurts worse initially than a broken heart.

But old pain, deep pain, pain that settles into your bones, goes silent—it hides, just like the past.

Lizzie was hiding something when she left. I know it now, deep down inside my core. She stole out of the house on the wind, quiet, because she didn't want to disturb me. She wanted to carry the secret away safely. But commotion followed, and it soon became chaos—my life was tossed into the air and left to land on its own in a new form.

Lizzie knew she would get me to do a handstand somehow. I just didn't expect it like this.

Chief doesn't yell when he sees my room. The whisper is worse.

"What the hell happened?"

"I'm concussed," I say. That doesn't work on Chief. "You said I should start painting again, so I did."

"I meant a canvas. Not your room. You've destroyed it."

"I think it looks good." Chief won't see the masterpiece, because I didn't make it for him. I painted for me. "Why did we move from Boise?" I ask.

"What?"

"Why did we leave?"

"I got a job in Spokane. Don't change the subject."

"You had a job in Boise."

"The police department in Spokane was a better fit for a single father." Chief keeps his eyes trained on the splattered walls. "I don't know how I'm going to fix this."

"It doesn't need to be fixed."

"You can't live in a room like this."

"Why not?"

"Because it's a complete mess."

"My life is a mess, and I live in it. What's so wrong with that?"

Chief doesn't appreciate that. "We need to fix this. Put it back into working order."

"Stop saving me." That gives him pause. "I'm not the victim here. I did this myself."

Chief is serious when he says, "If you're not the victim, that means you're the criminal."

"Cuff me." I hold out both of my arms. I know what it feels like to be bound and unmoving. Handcuffs are just a physical representation of my life before this summer. I don't need hands to kiss Luca anyway.

Chief huffs, exhausted. He needs his beers, and sleep, and to watch someone else solve a *Wheel of Fortune* puzzle. My mess has screwed up his predictable morning, but I won't apologize.

"Do you miss Boise?"

Chief groans. "Stop with the questions about Boise."

"Why?"

"Because it's in the past."

"And yet it affects the present. Maybe if you talked about it. Let the truth out—"

"Stop!" Chief yells, clearly overwhelmed. The whisper follows the shout. "I don't want to talk about it." He murmurs so softly, I think maybe I've imagined it. "If you want to be treated like a criminal, so be it. You're grounded. Again. This time no phone. No computer. No leaving the property. For a week. Jails don't always come with bars, Wren."

He takes my phone and laptop and leaves. But the past remains.

The mess that Chief sees is a masterpiece to me. It's the first real thing I've ever painted for no one but myself. And now I'm itching to paint more.

Luca's impression is still on my bed and ingrained in the floor, but he's gone. He left in the early hours of the morning, when the sun was just starting to show. We watched from the floor as the first rays hit the colors splashed on my walls.

"It's brilliant," Luca said.

But my mind was burning with a question. "When you look at me, what do you see?"

"Hotness." I shoved him playfully. "What? That's my answer. You're hot."

He saw my strength before I did. Maybe Luca could see my aura, too. Sometimes we're too in our heads to know what's true. Maybe all these years, I couldn't see an aura because I didn't want to. It was easier to believe something was wrong with me than to just *be* me.

"I mean it," I said. "Do you see anything?"

"Hold still," he said. So I did. I lay on the floor as Luca hovered over me, his hands skimming my entire body just centimeters above the skin, so I could feel his heat but not his touch. Shivers ran down my arms and legs. I'd never felt anything like it. For all the kissing and touching, the anticipation was more intense.

Luca let his mouth dangle over mine tauntingly. "I do notice something."

"What?"

It felt like we hung, suspended in the air.

"Love," he said. "I can feel it."

"I can feel it, too."

And then he kissed me like I held the energy he needed to get going. Then he tiptoed out of my house, leaving me breathless and happy. His aura matched the rays of sunshine in the sky as he swam through the air on his skateboard.

I looked at myself in the mirror. My reflection was barely visible through all the paint. My black hair hung tangled and knotted, and color was streaked all over my skin and clothes, but I looked closer. And I saw it.

Like a sheen on my skin, like a layer of sweat or the heat from a sunburn, a dim aura glowed shamrock green, fresh and alive.

Luca was right. The first signs of love had grown on me through the night.

Now even Chief's whisper can't ruin how I feel. He can tell me to clean up. He can paint my walls himself. He can throw out my stained sheets and ruined clothes, but I'll know what was there—what grew in my room the night Luca and I painted my walls and found meaning in ourselves.

You can lock a criminal up for life, but there are some things no one can steal.

I touch my swollen lips and still feel Luca's mouth on mine. Lying back on my bed, I stare at the ceiling. It's perfect.

Sometimes a person has to demolish what was to build what should be.

Is that what Chief did to our lives in Boise? Did he demolish his past so he could move on to the future? If so, I can't fault him, but I also can't stop wondering, Why leave Idaho? Why leave his friends, his job, the life he built? He was in love. He said himself that he never wanted anything more than my mom. That *she* did the leaving. But so did we. If he wanted her to find us, he'd have stayed put. Chief has chased enough criminals to know that to catch someone you have to follow them. People who want to escape turn the other way.

But escape from what?

The walls of my house are crumbling, and my place of reprieve is beginning to look like a prison. Is that how Lizzie felt from the start? Is that what Lizzie meant in her postcard? Did she figure it out and decide to break free? Does she want me to follow?

But where is she? How can I find her if she won't tell me where to go?

When Olga shows up for her shift later in the day, Chief fires her. She stands in the doorway, her purse slung over her arm, her expression blank. I'm standing behind him, ashamed that what I did lost Olga her job. She even made me soup.

"I trusted you to keep this house in order," Chief says.

"I've been coming here fourteen years," she says flatly. "I never miss a day. I'm always on time. I follow your rules."

"And I'm sorry to see you go, but all the same, I think this is for the best," he says.

Olga steps closer to him, pointing her finger in his face. "I've been looking after children for years. I see things. I know more. You think what you do is for the best, but that's where parents make mistake."

Chief is curt in his response. "What's that supposed to mean?"

"Your best?" Olga points at me. "Or her best?" It's the most I've ever seen her combat Chief. I want to apologize, tell her that this is all my fault, but my words fail me.

Chief rigidly hands Olga a check. "It covers two weeks' pay. Good luck."

As Olga walks out the front door, she says, "It was bound to happen at some point. That girl wasn't going to stay quiet forever, no matter how hard you try to make it so."

"It really was the best soup I've ever had," I say as Olga walks down the front steps. When she looks at me one last time, I know she wasn't sleeping last night when Luca snuck in. She sacrificed herself so I could live a little more.

I'm pretty sure she did the same for Lizzie.

Later that night, when the house is quiet, I realize that Olga's silence actually made a lot of noise. And I already miss it.

Chief takes the rest of the week off to make sure I adhere to my punishment. When I ask him what he's going to do about me when he goes back to work, he avoids an answer, saying only that he's got it covered.

I wash my sheets and clean up my room as well as I can, but the color stays. It's embedded, on the walls and furniture, under my fingernails. Chief can lock me up, but the color is here now. Even in me.

We watch *Wheel of Fortune* in silence. I sit on the couch with a new reality. For years I've blinded myself with other puzzles instead of realizing my life, this house, Chief, Lizzie—*we* are the puzzle no one wanted to solve. Until Lizzie did. I'm sure of that now.

Both Chief and I are hiding something. How he examines me, the soft way he pads around the house, the nonchalant questions and casual conversation—it's a game of hide-and-seek, though I'm not sure either of us is willing to find the other yet.

So we hide in whispers.

Chief can't seem to sleep through the night. I hear him walking the hallways, getting water in the kitchen, watching television. Something keeps him awake. He sleeps only in spurts—a few hours here and a few hours there, never really rested, always on alert. Like he's worried I'm going to leave, too. Or that something might come back to haunt us.

But it's already back. I can feel it.

I walk the steps into the dark basement during one of Chief's afternoon naps.

In some places, make-believe isn't possible. Lizzie's words echo in my mind.

I need to see her.

Boxes are stacked in the darkest corner of the basement, where the cobwebs are thick and the spiders play. I brush them aside, digging through winter gear and holiday decorations and old DVDs. The unmarked boxes of pictures are way in the back.

When I finally get to the photos, I'm covered in dust and dirt, my hair tangled with cobwebs, my fingers grimy. But no one comes to a precipice clean. To reach the edge of a cliff, one has to crawl, hands and knees, to the ledge. To peer over slowly.

That's how I open the box. Slowly.

I'm not sure what I expected. What does love look like locked in a basement? Part of me wanted an organized scrapbook, or delicately handled photo albums. How love *should* be touched. But love doesn't work that way. It's dirty and messy and unpredictable, and sometimes, when it becomes too much, it gets tossed to the back of the basement under the assumption that it will always be there when we need it.

Luca and I know better. No one expects their memories to leave, and so we treat them poorly, casting moments aside in arrogance when we should be cradling them.

I don't find her immediately. My heart pounds as I peel through the pictures of me and Lizzie and Chief, our early life in Spokane—Chief in his police uniform on Christmas Day, Lizzie's first day of kindergarten, Chief visiting her classroom. Me on a swing next to Chloe. A Fourth of July barbecue in her backyard. I see a tuna casserole on the potluck table, and I can't help but laugh.

For a moment I'm distracted. Old pictures will do that.

I dig deeper into the box, the dust making me sneeze. Lizzie and I knew that finding our mom wouldn't be easy or clean. It would hurt, scrape, bruise the skin, and tear up our clothes. So we painted a clean life.

I pull another picture from the mess, and I see her. My mom has my hair—dark, practically jet black—and green eyes like mine. In fact, everything about her is me. For my entire life I've assumed she looked like Lizzie, with brown, flowing hair and eyes of the earth, skin of the sun. That she loved Lizzie because they were the same. That she gave Lizzie the sun, and me nothing, because unlike flowers, a child will grow even if you don't water it.

But I am a replica of her.

Footsteps sound from upstairs. I close the box quickly, putting it back where it belongs. Then I see a sweater, green with embroidered flowers around the collar.

Lizzie said that it felt like she was wearing a garden.

"It's like I'm tangled in flowers, Songbird. Doesn't that sound lovely?" she said when she found the sweater at a thrift store this past spring. "Where do you think this hole came from?" she asked, holding up a pair of jeans too big for her with tears in the knees.

I never knew.

"Skydiving?" she asked.

"That's too scary."

"Professional wrestler?"

"No one wrestles in jeans," I said. "Someone probably just tripped and fell. That's the story."

"No, Songbird. The real story is what they were running from."

I pick up Lizzie's sweater. She was down here recently. Not long before she left.

"Wren?" Chief's voice carries down the stairs. I put the picture in my pocket but leave the sweater, and I race upstairs before he can figure out that I was digging through our dirty past.

35

GRAND THEFT AUTO

Chief is taking another afternoon nap. I'm roller-skating in circles in the driveway, practicing my crossovers, when Baby Girl arrives.

I can tell the instant I see her that something is wrong.

"Did something happen with Leia?" I ask.

Baby Girl shakes her head. Fatigue clings to her like a wet blanket. "She's working today. So is Luca. He's different. I can see it." That makes me smile. "I think he finally stopped running from himself."

"It was getting tiring."

She exhales a breath that says, *I know this with every inch of whoever I am.*

"You know the problem with carousel horses?" she asks.

"What?"

"They don't go anywhere when you need them to."

"This is true."

"It never bothered me until now. And if I have to listen to that song one more time, I'm going to scream. I think I need a new job."

"OK."

"Also, I like chai-tea lattes. I can't stop drinking them. They're my favorite."

"That's great."

Baby Girl runs a hand over her freshly shaved head. "And I like not having hair."

"You look good with a shaved head."

She nods. "I hate skinny jeans and the sound of corduroy pants rubbing together and the saying 'Your vibe attracts your tribe.' It's insulting. And I think I want to major in psychology. I figure I know a lot about people, seeing as I've tried on so many personalities."

"You're making real progress, Baby Girl."

"Thanks," she says. "But that's not why I'm here."

She has a hard time saying what comes next. The words lodge in her throat. I've seen the look so many times on Chief.

"Luca told me about your room," she says.

"Chief wasn't happy. I may have gone a bit overboard."

"Sometimes the only option is to jump ship," she says.

"Chief doesn't see it that way."

"That's because he's the captain of the vessel. His job is to save you."

"I don't need saving."

"Would you prefer he let you drown?"

"But what if the ship is sinking? What if getting off is how to survive?"

"Well, maybe you have it backward. Maybe Chief needs *you* to save him. The captain is supposed to go down with the ship. Maybe you need to convince him to screw the rules and jump with you."

I never thought of it like that.

"You definitely should major in psychology," I say. "You're good at it."

"Thanks."

Whatever Baby Girl needs to say comes closer to the surface.

"What is it?" I ask.

Finally she says, "I need your help." She exhales a long breath. "My dad . . . He's dying."

"What?" I spit out.

"Turns out, the reason he didn't show up for our last meeting is because he's in the hospital with stage-four lung cancer. My mom refuses to see him. She says he deserves to die on his own. She won't take me there either."

"Where is he?"

"Coeur d'Alene."

That's forty minutes away.

"What about Leia? She has a car."

"I can't ask her."

"Did something happen between you two?"

"No, but she doesn't know"—Baby Girl looks at the ground, ashamed, and my heart aches—"what you know about my past. And I don't want to tell her."

"Why not?"

"Because no matter how many times I tell myself it wasn't my fault, a little voice in the back of my head tells me it was. And I'm worried that if I tell her, she'll feel the same way and see me differently."

I understand.

"It wasn't your fault," I say softly.

"That's beside the point at the moment. My mom's probably right. My dad *does* deserve to die alone, but death is rarely about the dying. I'm not sure I can live with myself if I don't at least see him one more time. Even if he is a horrible person. Every *body* needs one asshole. And he was mine. I need to say goodbye."

Chief will probably be up soon, patrolling the house again.

"And you're sure he's going to die?"

"It's an inevitability for all, Wren, but it's imminent for him."

"Do you want to borrow the cruiser?"

"I don't know how to drive. I was a pothead for most of my junior year. Not conducive for driving . . . and then I just kind of forgot."

"So you want me to drive you."

Baby Girl gives me a look of guilt, and of hope. "You said if I ever need you . . ."

I've only ever driven a go-cart. And I managed to get a concussion. "I'll do it."

"Really?"

"People only die once," I say. "That's worth stealing a car for."

The hospital smells like sterile cotton balls. Baby Girl visits her dad while I sit in the hallway. I offered to go in with her, but she said honesty doesn't like observers. She needs to do this alone.

I keep telling myself that, technically, I didn't steal the car, since it's mine and we plan to return it immediately.

Minutes tick by, and then an hour. I don't know when someone becomes OK with leaving a dying person. Walking away means never seeing him again. A final goodbye shouldn't be rushed.

But I don't regret helping Baby Girl. She needs me, and up until this summer I'd never felt that before.

Three hours later she emerges. No tears stain her cheeks, though she looks a little pale.

"Let's go to Denny's," she says.

So that's where I take Baby Girl after she's said goodbye to her dad for the last time.

We slide into the sticky booth and take our sticky menus from the waitress. She leaves two glasses of water. We didn't talk as we drove to the restaurant. The air-conditioning in the cruiser doesn't work, so we rolled down the windows and let the wind talk for us.

"Moons Over My Hammy?" I ask.

Baby Girl is distracted. "I ordered that only because my dad did, but it always grossed me out. I choked it down for him. I'm not that hungry, actually." She takes a deep breath.

I get it. Death has a way of consuming people.

The waitress comes back, notepad in hand. "What would you like to order?"

"Nothing," Baby Girl says.

"Why come to a restaurant, then?"

"To look at the menu," Baby Girl says to the waitress. "I have options now."

The waitress turns to me, disgruntled.

"I don't have any money," I say with a sorry expression.

"Enjoy your free water." The waitress leaves us then.

"So . . . will you miss . . . Moons Over My Hammy?" I ask.

"I'd like to say no, but people miss hate as much as they miss love. Both leave irreparable marks." Baby Girl peruses the menu. "You can't forget the taste. You know what I mean?"

"Well . . . you could never eat at a Denny's again if you don't want to."

Baby Girl sits back in her seat. "I don't want to live like that, Wren. Avoiding . . . I think that's what I've done most of my life."

More minutes pass without words. A container of crayons sits on our table. I ask the hostess for paper. When I sit back down, I draw a tic-tac-toe board.

"*Xs* or *Os*?" I ask Baby Girl.

"I'll be *Xs*."

The first round ends in a cat's game. I draw another board, and we come to the same end. Then another and another, each round ending in a draw.

"I think we're too old for this game," Baby Girl says. "Neither of us can win."

"It's not about winning. It's just a good distraction."

"Well, in that case . . ." She makes another tic-tac-toe board. Slowly the paper is filled with distractions.

"Isn't it weird that we require a class and multiple tests to drive but anyone can be a parent?" she asks, placing an *X* in the center box.

"Chief always says a car is a weapon." I add an *O*.

She puts an *X* in the upper-right corner. "So is parenting."

I can't think of anything to say. She is right.

We end another game in a tie.

The waitress comes back over. "Are you going to eat or what? My shift's about to end."

"What's the most popular thing on the menu?" Baby Girl asks.

"Moons Over My Hammy."

Baby Girl looks at me. "Figures."

"You can't just sit here all day."

"Yes, I can," Baby Girl says. "You're open twenty-four seven. I could live here if I wanted to."

"Why would you want to live at Denny's?" the waitress asks. "This place is a shithole."

A smirk pulls at Baby Girl's cheeks. "Maybe that's why my asshole dad brought me here. He felt at home."

And then Baby Girl starts laughing uncontrollably, like a volcano has erupted from her gut and won't stop until her insides have calmed again. Tears streak her face as she tosses her head back, cackling. I've never seen her like this. Laughter shatters her into beautiful pieces, right here in life's shithole.

The waitress doesn't realize that she's seeing a girl's becoming, right in front of our eyes. In the middle of death and shit, Baby Girl pulls herself from the wreckage.

When the laughter has subsided, the tears on Baby Girl's skin give her a new, fresh glow, her eyes shimmering with a light I've never seen before. She says to the waitress, "I'm ready to leave now. Thanks for the water."

We get back in the cruiser, windows down, and leave Denny's. Baby Girl has this serene look to her.

"I think I want to get my own apartment near campus, or live in a dorm. Maybe next week, you, me, and Leia can go shopping together?"

"Sure," I say.

"And I'm going to tell her. About my dad. Because she should know."

"I think that's a good idea."

A few minutes pass before Baby Girl says, "Thank you, Wren."

I don't know what to say.

"I told him I forgive him," she says.

"You did?"

She nods slowly. "Not for him. For me." She's practically floating above the seat, the lightest I've ever seen her, like each of her costumes has been stripped away and all that's left is her real skin. No hiding. "If I didn't forgive him, he'd always have control over me. He'd be *my* story. Even after he dies. I didn't want that. But now . . . for the first time in my life, I feel free."

"Lizzie always said freedom is a noun, not a verb," I say. "You can't *do* freedom. You have to *be* it."

She closes her eyes and soaks up the sunshine. A glow settles around her, a beautiful, radiant shade of light purple.

"Orchid," I say.

"What?"

"Your aura is orchid."

Baby Girl smiles, and I return the look. Moments pass like the wind floating through the car.

"Lizzie should be here," Baby Girl says. Her tone has shifted. A shadow blocks the sun and cools the car. "Wren?"

"Yeah?"

"You know how my dad gave me money every month?"

"Yes."

"It always felt . . . dirty, so I never spent it. I just saved it up."

"Are you going to spend it now?"

I can't keep my eyes simultaneously on her and the road.

"I gave it to Lizzie," she says.

My foot comes off the gas. "What?"

"I gave her the money so she could leave."

A siren slices through our conversation. In my rearview mirror blue and red lights swirl. It pulls something from the deep.

A memory.

Sing something, Songbird, Lizzie's tiny voice begged. *Distract me from the visions that like to tell different stories at night.*

Don't worry, Lizzie. The sun never really goes away.

I need you to remind me.

Lizzie took my hand in her cold palm, and I began to sing.

You are my sunshine . . .

"Wren." Baby Girl's voice sings in my ears along with the song, and the vision of Lizzie dissolves into the wind. I gently press the brake and pull the cruiser to the side of the road safely. Parked, we wait, Baby Girl and I frozen in our seats.

An officer approaches the car.

Baby Girl whispers, "I'm sorry I lied to you."

Chloe's dad appears at the window. "Get out of the car, Wren. You're under arrest."

36

NO MORE PRETENDING

Before Chloe's dad dropped off Baby Girl at her house, I whispered to her, "What about a name? I think it's time you start thinking of a name other than Baby Girl."

"Aren't you mad at me? I'm so sorry, Wren."

"Just focus on you."

"What about Lizzie?"

But it wasn't the time to discuss that. We were locked in a cage in the back of a police cruiser.

Here at home, the veins in Chief's neck are already pulsing when I walk through the door, trailing behind Mr. Dillingham.

I'm starting to think my life might be one proverbial birdcage, made by the hands of Chief.

"Thanks, Phil." Chief keeps his cool for the moment.

"Not a problem," Mr. Dillingham says. "See you at the game."

Once it's just Chief and me, the coolness is gone.

"First you break curfew, then destroy your room, and now this," Chief says. "What the hell is going on?"

"Baby Girl needed me," I say.

"For what?"

"Moons Over My Hammy."

"You broke the law to go to Denny's? Are you out of your mind?"

"I wish. I'm so far *in* my mind, I'm not sure if what I'm looking at is real or not."

"Driving without a license is dangerous," he says. "How many times have I told you? Cars are weapons. They kill more people than guns."

"Staying on a sinking ship will kill you, too."

"What are you talking about?"

"Some laws are worth breaking in the moment," I say.

"No," Chief says definitively. "If we all thought like that, there would be anarchy."

"What's wrong with a little mayhem?"

Chief huffs. "Laws are in place to protect people, Wren. You need to follow them."

"Screw the rules, Chief." And then I beg, "Jump off this sinking ship with me."

But the argument is fruitless. We won't get anywhere. Chief and I are in a game of tic-tac-toe, both of us too smart to lose, so we just keep building a new game, putting up walls, containing each move.

"Go to your room," he says.

"Fine," I say. "But you can't keep me locked up forever."

Eventually there's a winner or someone walks away from the game.

Wilder is back. This time he's in my room. It's so dark outside, time seems not to exist.

"This is spiraling out of control," he says.

"I know. I can feel it."

209

"There's still time to stop it."

"I don't think so, Wilder."

"You can't handle this. You're weak."

"No," I say firmly.

"Yes," he says just as firmly. "You're broken. You'll always be broken."

"That doesn't mean I'm weak." My words come out softer than I want.

He paces my room, his steps heavy, intrusive. "Look at the mess you made. And it's only getting worse."

"It's not a mess."

"Yes, it is," he says.

I clench my fists. "I think it's beautiful."

"You're not thinking straight, Wren. You can't be trusted. Anyone who came in here would see a mess. You're fooling yourself."

"Luca didn't think so."

"We've been over this. He's going to leave you."

"He loves me, and I love him."

"Chief loved your mom, and look what happened," Wilder says. "I'm trying to help. Let's be honest. You're weird, Wren. You always have been. You were born that way. You don't belong, and you never will."

"I'm not listening to you." I cover my ears.

"You can't shut me up that easily."

"Go away."

"Make me."

Wilder stands in front of the window, where I stood when I first saw him. With a perfect view of his bedroom. The night shades his body, making him seem practically one with the dark. But I'm not the girl who turned her light on and invited him in anymore. I'm different.

"See," Wilder says. "You can't. You're not strong enough to get rid of me."

My body tenses with anger and frustration.

"Don't do this to me, Wren," he says.

"I have to."

"No, you don't. There's still time. You made this. You can change it back to the way it was. It was good, just you and me. Remember? We felt safe. It can be like that again. It's not too late."

"It *is* too late."

"This will be the end of us. Are you prepared for that?"

I can't answer him.

"You're so messed up, you don't even know what's real," he says. "You might even be crazy. What do you think people will do when they find out? They'll leave you. No one will want you. Do you actually think you're different? You're not. This will end with you alone. Like it always does."

"Stop!" I yell, my eyes pinched closed and tears streaming down my cheeks. "I'm not listening to you anymore. I have to try. Even if I fail."

"How could you do this to me?" Wilder whispers. "To us?"

"Leave. Now."

"You're not strong enough, Wren. You need me."

My heart pounds in my chest, heavy and fast. I muster the courage to look at him through my tears.

"We're not the same," I say. "You don't have an aura, and you never will."

"Don't do this," he pleads.

This is the hardest truth about love. It's the ugly, the broken, the messy side. The loneliest side.

But I listen to this truth with everything that I am.

It is easy to love someone else. The harder task is loving yourself.

"I *am* strong."

A breeze whistles through my window.

And Wilder is gone.

I look at myself in the mirror, my shamrock-green aura radiant, and take a few steps back. That's what Lizzie said I needed to do to see the picture clearly.

There before me, just like Baby Girl said, I see myself reflected back, surrounded by a mess I made, tears streaming down my face.

But through the disarray, looking right at me is what I've been waiting to see.

Love.

37

STRIKE THREE

It's the last softball game of the season. Every family member is invited to play. Chief's tuna casserole sits on the potluck table, sweating in the sun along with french-onion dip, fried chicken, watermelon, and an untouched vegetable platter. Flies land on the food, though even the bugs avoid the broccoli. Just like last year and the year before. It's as if nothing has changed, except everything has changed.

I've decided to play. It surprised the hell out of Chief when I came downstairs in sport shorts and a tank top.

In years past Lizzie and I would opt out to pick bouquets of dandelions. Making crowns felt better than making home runs. She'd take my arm and rub the dandelion on my skin, painting it yellow. "See, Songbird? You have sunshine in you. All you have to do is paint it true."

I would let Lizzie rub dandelion all over—my face, my arms, my legs—until I was covered in yellow and sneezing. Mrs. Dillingham, eying my dandelion stains, would whisper to the other ladies about our "eccentricities" and how girls raised by single fathers show the lack of a mother in their actions.

Chief made me take a shower the moment we got home. The yellow disappeared down the drain. The canvas became blank again, until Lizzie painted the truth on my skin again the next summer.

Now I rub a dandelion along my arm, a streak of yellow appearing, and then look at the bright sun. Streaks of light are everywhere now. I'm alive. I squint in the brightness, but it's time for eyes wide open.

At some point every artist stops. A last brushstroke, and the painting is complete. There is no going back, and the only way of moving forward is to tell a new story on a blank canvas.

Once you've painted the truth, you have to live with the masterpiece. I brush another line of yellow on my skin.

"Wren!" Chief's voice startles me. He waves me toward the dugout. The inning is over, and it's our turn to bat.

Running is easy now. Muscles have formed that I didn't have at the start of summer. I'm still wobbly on my skates, and I know it's going to hurt getting knocked down in Roller Derby, but it's what I want. Pain is a part of progress.

Even Chloe sees a change in me. She eyes me suspiciously as we run past each other. It's graveyard shift versus day shift, and we're playing on opposite teams. When I asked Chief who's keeping Spokane safe while we play softball, he said, "Rookies."

Today would be a good day to get arrested.

Chloe came up to me before the game, her blond hair in a braid that hung down her back.

"You stole a car?" she said accusatorily. "Are you crazy?"

"Maybe. And technically, I didn't steal anything. It's my car." Chief has it parked at the police station now. He's uncertain he'll ever give it back to me.

"What were you and Baby Girl doing?"

"None of your business." I haven't told Chief the truth. I wasn't about to tell Chloe.

"You're seriously not going to tell me."

Her belief that she *should* be privy to that information is exactly what's wrong with Chloe. She hasn't earned the right to know about Baby Girl's dad. She hasn't earned the right to know how Baby Girl found freedom in death and shit.

What Baby Girl said about her dad echoed in my memory. *Every body needs an asshole.* Turns out, Chloe is mine.

"Why are you laughing?" Chloe demanded, running an insecure hand over her clothes and face.

"Nothing."

Chloe kept puckering her lips petulantly. Her mouth looked like an *asshole, asshole, asshole.* I couldn't hold back the giggles.

"Stop it!" She actually stomped.

But it was funny. It was like someone took the cork out of our relationship after it had been shaken up all summer, and now it was exploding everywhere. Unstoppable. Overflowing. Never to be contained again. It was over.

"It's not polite to laugh at people, Wren. Didn't your *mom* teach you that?" The laughter stopped. I choked. "That's right. You don't *have* a mom." She walked away.

Now we pass each other again as the teams switch out. She glares at me. She has no clue what an asshole she really is.

The sun comes and goes as puffy clouds pass through the sky. With the shade comes a gentle breeze.

The game is tied in the fifth—three to three. Unsurprisingly, Chief is our team captain. He calls out the batting order for the inning. He has a clipboard with the Spokane Recreational Softball rules, which he checks repeatedly.

I'm fourth in the batting order this inning. So far I've been up to the plate twice, both strikeouts. Chief seemed unsurprised, but as I walked back, bat dragging on the ground, he patted my shoulder and offered words of encouragement. And critique.

"Next time keep your eye on the ball."

"You're swinging just a second too late."

"Choke up on the bat, Wren."

"Don't crowd the plate."

Officer McGhee bats first, and he hits a single.

Savannah Walsh, a girl in junior high whose mom runs dispatch, bats next. She's tagged out on her way to first.

Mrs. Marlow strikes out.

Chief hollers, "You're up, Wren."

I move toward the plate sluggishly. Chief now stands just behind me.

"Remember what I said: Keep your eye on the ball. Bend your knees. Swing from the hip."

The pitcher narrows his eyes. My team cheers from the dugout. Chloe stands in left field, her stance arrogant, her arms crossed as if she's sure I can't hit a ball all the way out there. But she doesn't know that I've spent the summer training to kick ass.

The first pitch comes. The softball lobs through the air. I swing, but no contact.

"That's OK." Chief claps behind me. "Now you know what it looks like."

I adjust my stance.

"A little wider," he says. I step my feet apart slightly. "Choke up, Wren."

My hands move slightly up the neck of the bat.

"Now, watch the ball."

The pitch is thrown. I keep my feet steady, my hands properly gripped, my eye trained. When the bat hits nothing but air, I'm almost knocked over. Chief catches me before I face-plant. Chloe's laughter arrives from the outfield, bringing my blood to a boiling point. She plays with her braid, smoothing her hand down her corn-silk hair as if it's a horse's mane.

"Try it again," Chief says. I yank my arm out of his grasp.

"Stop telling me *how* to play the game, and just let me play it," I insist.

"I'm just trying to give you some pointers," he says. "To help you out."

"I don't need your help," I say, grabbing the bat from the dirt. "I can handle this."

"Like you've handled everything else this summer?"

He has no idea. Chief is too weighed down with rules and laws and handcuffs. He restrains people because he's scared. I thought it was because that's his job, but Lizzie knew the truth. He's screaming scared inside.

But this isn't the time to fight with Chief. That time will come, but it's not today. The yellow streak on my arm catches my attention. The truth must be painted, but piece by piece, brushstroke by brushstroke.

The pitch comes. The arch is high and off center. It's a definite ball, but I'm desperate to hit it—desperate to prove to Chief that I can do this—and I don't care about the rules. Hitting something will feel so much better than standing around waiting.

"Don't swing!" Chief yells.

I go for it.

The crack of contact shudders through me.

"Run!" Chief yells.

I take off toward first base. The ball soars into left field, where Chloe is standing, playing with her hair. I pause at first, long enough to see Chloe picking up the ball, completely shocked. Someone yells for her to throw it. But she holds on to it. Our eyes connect.

She doesn't want to give up the chance to get me out herself.

I take off toward second base.

Chloe runs toward it from the outfield.

Chief screams, "Go back to first, Wren! Go back to first! Just stay put!"

But staying still is no longer an option. Staying still won't paint the story. Hiding the colors in the basement doesn't mean they're not there. I can't stop now.

Chloe's dad is yelling, too. "Throw the damn ball, Chloe! What the hell are you doing?"

But this isn't about the game. We near second base from opposite sides. I know I'm going to make it first, but Chloe looks determined, and she spent the summer at CrossFit with Jay, banging tires and swinging kettlebells and drinking protein shakes. I know the look—all the times she's bossed me around, all the times she made me feel like I should be grateful for her friendship, like I should think her existence is one big favor to me.

I told Leia weeks ago that I didn't think I was strong enough to knock someone over. But that has changed. Physical pain pales in comparison to the pain of an empty room in your heart.

Chloe's bright-red aura tints my vision. All I see is her blinding, bleeding selfishness.

I dive at the bag. My knee scrapes on the dirt. Chloe does the same. Our bodies collide and tangle.

And then I see it—the ball is loose. Chloe dropped it. I scramble back to the base and touch it with my hand. Then I stand and stamp my foot down.

Dirty and bleeding, I win.

"Did you see that!" Chloe screams. "She ran right into me!"

"You ran into *me*!"

Chief, Mr. Dillingham, *and* Mrs. Dillingham run onto the field.

"She's insane! She attacked me!" Chloe screams. "What the hell is wrong with you, Wren?"

"What's wrong with *me*?"

"Calm down, girls," Mr. Dillingham says. Chief searches his clipboard for the proper rule.

"I'm sure there's some procedure outlined in the Spokane Recreational Softball rules for just this kind of thing," he says.

"Yeah," Chloe snaps at me. "Don't play with *crazy* people. Did you see how she came at me? She's taking her jealousy out on me, Mom."

"You know I pride myself on staying out of other people's business," Mrs. Dillingham chides. "But we all know Wren's been off this summer. Chloe has a point."

"What?" both Chief and I bite back at the exact same time.

"Look, Wren, I'm sorry that I have a *boyfriend*." Chloe tosses her hair. "I'm sorry that I have a *life*. But what did you expect? You're moving to Utah. I *had* to find new friends."

"Chloe," Mr. Dillingham snaps.

His wife is silent.

I can't seem to breathe. Like the morning I woke up and found Lizzie gone. As if the rotation of the planet stopped, making the wind die, the sky fall. My lungs stop working, only for a moment but enough to shake my center clear off balance.

I look at Chief. "What?"

"We'll talk about this later." Chief is looking at his clipboard, like a coward.

Mr. Dillingham whispers, loudly enough for me to hear. "Chloe, I told you that in confidence. You weren't supposed to say anything."

In an unapologetic tone, Chloe says, "Oops."

How indelicately she treats my life.

"That was your plan all along," I say to Chief. "You're sending me away."

"We'll talk about this later."

I'm trapped. Lizzie was, too.

She was getting out of Spokane only if Chief let her go. If she found something that forced his hand. She didn't sneak out a locked door. He opened it.

I can't believe I didn't realize this before.

"You know where she is," I say. "You've known the whole time."

I take off running. Chief doesn't follow. He knows I'm trying to escape a labyrinth. There is no getting out. I have no car. No phone. No money. He's the police. He'll find me. Chief will see to that. I can run all over Spokane, but in the end I'll come back to my house and he'll close the door. Chief has made it so.

The truth is this: I am the songbird. And Chief is the cage.

38

A KISS TO BUILD A DREAM ON

Luca and I are sheltered under the bus stop outside Happy Homes Assisted Living Center. Rain drips on the glass, smearing its way down to the ground. The wind picks up, and a few dried leaves gather in a swirl.

"Fall is coming," I say. A chill rolls down my arms.

I ran to Luca's house. I told him about Utah. About Baby Girl and the money she gave to Lizzie. About Chief, and about how Lizzie disappeared because my dad opened the door, on purpose. And he didn't tell me. And he didn't go after her.

Luca said there was only one place we should go. In the dark of night, nothing can be solved. All we can do is wait for the bus to come.

"It's still summer," Luca says. "Let's not think about fall."

"I think I hear sirens. Chief's coming for me."

"That's just the wind howling." Luca pulls me in closer. "Don't worry. The bus will be here soon, and we'll get out of here."

"Where are we going, Luca?"

"New York City," he says. "We'll get a loft in Brooklyn where you can paint, and I can skateboard at the park down the street."

"We can get restaurant jobs."

"Or work at a coffee shop."

"And live off of free lattes and scones."

"Caffeine and carbs. Does a person need anything else? You can go to the art museum on your days off."

"We'll drink wine and wear black and always look slightly disgruntled, even though we're blissfully happy . . ." I pause. "Will you miss it here?"

"No way." But Luca is lying. I can tell.

"I hear it gets pretty cold in New York in the winter," I say.

"And the heat in the summer makes the city stink."

"Maybe we should go to California instead."

"But the traffic is awful."

"And I'm not fancy enough for LA."

"Texas sounds interesting," Luca offers. "I hear everything's bigger down there."

"I like us just the size we are."

"Florida has the ocean. Or we could eat lobster in Boston."

"Chicago dyes its river green on Saint Patrick's Day."

"We could hike the Appalachian Trail," he says. "Or get a houseboat and float down the Mississippi? That sounds nice."

But it won't work. I can't pretend the truth away anymore.

"I'd miss when the lilacs bloom here in the spring," I say.

"Me, too." Luca pulls me into him. I rest my head on his shoulder. "It's a good thing the bus isn't here yet. We have time to decide."

He reaches around me protectively, as if he can prevent what's going to happen. But it's all make-believe, the lies we tell ourselves to make living better. No matter how close Luca hugs me, I can't shake the feeling that I'm near the end of the picture. It's almost clear. Just a few more steps backward.

I nuzzle into Luca's neck and smell his familiar scent. Even after I washed my sheets, the memory of him clung to each fiber. If I could disappear into his skin right now, I'd do it.

I won't slip away again. I won't let myself go. I'm stronger than that.

"Is life just a made-up story?" I ask him. "An imagined daydream and night-dream, until it's over?"

"If that's the case," he whispers, "we can be anything we want."

I turn toward him. "All I want is to be with you right now."

Luca kisses me. The chill of the rainy night dissipates around us. He tangles his hands through my hair, like roots burrowing in the ground. Grabbing at his T-shirt, I pull him closer, drinking him in.

This is life in a kiss. My life. Held between his lips, whispered in my name.

And yet something is dying. Withering away. The part of me that liked being in a cage. The part of me that found comfort in being unwanted. The part of me that lived a lie I told myself.

I kiss Luca with everything that I am—with lips and tongue, hands and arms and skin and bones, heart and soul. Seconds that quickly become minutes to wrap myself in the truth I've created before shedding light on the lies around me.

Thunder claps, and I shudder, pulling back from Luca.

He kisses my forehead. The rain falls harder now. Water cascades in sheets down the glass, like we're under a waterfall. Hidden.

"Let's never leave here," I say.

"Don't worry. The bus won't come. We're safe."

"For now," I say. "Until we decide we can't wait any longer."

"Or until we forget why we sat down in the first place."

"I don't ever want to forget you."

"Then you know what you have to do," Luca says.

"I have to leave here, don't I?"

He pulls me back into him. "Not until morning. No one should go out in this rain."

"OK. We'll wait until the rain stops."

"What should we do to pass the time?"

"I could sing to you," I suggest.

Luca smiles. "You know how to sing?"

"One song."

He lies down on the bench and puts his head in my lap. I stroke his hair, my fingers memorizing each strand.

"It's a song about sunshine."

"I think I know this one," he says. "OK, Songbird. Sing."

So I do.

And when I'm done, Luca asks me to sing it again and again and again, until the rain departs and a slice of morning peeks out from the horizon.

"Your singing worked," Luca says, his voice hoarse. "The sun is back. I think it's time."

"I know. I can feel it."

"Do you need to borrow my belief in you again?"

"No," I say. "I've found my own strength now."

He kisses my forehead. "It was there all along."

"Can I have your phone?" I ask.

He takes it from his pocket. My heart beats quickly. My mind clouds with what-ifs, but going back is not an option. The time for fantasy is over.

I search for Vivienne Rhine. The truth was here all along, like the little secrets tucked in the books in the Spokane Public Library. That's the odd thing with the truth. Just because you can't see it doesn't mean it isn't there.

Luca must see it on my face. "Is it what you thought?"

"Yes."

"Boise?"

This feels impossible. "Yes."

"Then we can find her."

"Yes."

Of all the scenarios Lizzie and I dreamed up, this is one I never expected.

"What is it?" he begs, touching my leg. "Tell me, Wren. Is there more?"

"Luca . . ." The sun has risen, painting the entirety of the bus stop in yellow. "There's so much more."

39

A MILLION PIECES OF LOVE

I stand in the kitchen, rain from the night before still softening my clothes. My knee is scabbed over from yesterday's softball game, the blood dried and cracked. It feels unfathomable that my fight with Chloe was just yesterday. I am living a new life today. Chloe feels so small—a pin drop—compared to this.

I walk through the house as if seeing it for the first time.

When I get upstairs, I find Lizzie lying in the hammock, surrounded by the forest on the walls.

She's a figment of my imagination, a set memory. Lizzie's wearing her worn-out, secondhand bell-bottom jeans with the holes in the knees, thumbing the scar from when she broke her leg, as if feeling to make sure she still exists underneath her clothes. That scar is her only flaw in a sea of perfection, and somehow it makes her even more beautiful.

The brown of her eyes matches the brown of her hair, features I thought were our mother's. Lizzie's frame is thin, but her ability to take up a room is unmatched, her cadmium-yellow aura radiant, even now in my fantasy. The aura is so warm, so like Luca's, that I wrap myself in it, finding the courage I need in the light.

This is so familiar, and yet it's as if I'm seeing Lizzie for the first time.

She cradles a cat in her lap.

I've been waiting for you, Songbird. Come here. Let me place love in your arms. Lizzie nuzzles the cat and whispers, *If we grab on to the pieces, one day we'll feel whole again. I promise.*

Quietly I take a seat next to my sister.

"I've missed you," I say.

I've missed you, too. Did you get my postcards?

Nodding, I take in the trees and flowers and butterflies. "I get it now. You didn't want to ruin the story."

We can make life anything we want if we pretend hard enough. Lizzie's eyes dance along with mine, along the world stuck, unmoving on the wall. *It's always summertime here. No one needs to be disappointed when winter comes. It's better to live here, Songbird.*

"Is it?"

But even Lizzie won't answer that.

"You didn't like to sleep," I say.

Lizzie pets the cat in her lap. *I'm hyperactive. You know that.*

"You hated cars."

It's not normal for a human body to travel that fast. We should stick to walking. Why must we be in a hurry?

"Chief always says that cars are weapons. They can kill people. Now I know why."

Let's not talk about depressing things. Paint me more flowers instead.

"You let me believe you were just like our mom. Even after you saw the picture of her."

I'm the wild child, just like her. I can't help but misbehave. But you, Songbird, you're such a good daughter. You would never let us down. Do you think my forest needs more insects? Maybe a caterpillar or two?

"I see it now, Lizzie," I say. "You were playing a part. But you saw things that weren't there. You worked every day to distract yourself. You told yourself it wasn't real. You painted a different life for us."

Sing me that song again, Songbird. How does it go?

"You looked at the world differently because you *had* to. Because if you didn't, you'd remember."

Lizzie sings to the cat lovingly. *You are my sunshine . . .*

"It won't work, Lizzie. Not this time."

Come on, Songbird, if you won't paint, at least try a handstand. It'll help. Turn this story upside down. You'll feel better.

"No. I'm done with handstands, Lizzie."

She gets up from the hammock, her long brown hair dangling down her back. She spins in circles, one after another after another. *Let's play our game. Where is she today? A lumber worker in Forks, but secretly she's a vampire killer. Or catching king crab off the coast of Alaska, sleeping on a boat, and popping Dramamine for seasickness. Or a samba dancer in Brazil, and she's in love with a man named Gabriel, who has a three-legged dog named Victor that likes to wear human clothes.*

"Stop it, Lizzie!" I grab her tightly, holding her still. "It won't work. Nothing will work anymore. It's over."

Don't say that, Songbird.

"It has to be. We can't go back."

Her eyes fill with tears. *But sadness is just so . . . sad.*

"But it's real, Lizzie. I can't keep living a lie."

Lizzie's cheeks are wet. Tears drip from her chin onto her clothes. *It's just so awful that the older we get, the more our imagination dies. I didn't want it to end this way. I wanted to save you from the sadness. I wanted us to live here in perpetual summer.*

"But you couldn't save yourself. You couldn't stop yourself from seeing the truth."

Lizzie shakes her head.

"So you left," I say. The cat walks around us, purring, its warm fur on our legs. "You could have collected a million pieces of love, but it still wouldn't have changed what happened to you. To us. It wouldn't have changed Mom. Not even love can protect memories." Then I say what is needed to move on. "I love you, Lizzie, but you don't have to protect me anymore. I can do this on my own."

Lizzie shatters in my mind. A breeze moves through the room, taking the tiny slivers of my fantasy away to dance and get lost in the painted trees and butterflies.

A noise down the hall catches my attention. Chief, with wet hair and a tired face, finds me in Lizzie's room. The fresh scent of a shower follows him in.

Everything is different. Most of all, Chief.

His face hangs heavy with fatigue, the gray circles under his eyes like sandbags, aging a man who should still be young. Who should be strong. Who should be a lot of things.

I see Chief for who he truly is. All those mornings solving puzzles, thinking I was sitting next to a father who wanted to know the answer, who *had* the answer, who solved crimes, who helped people. He was justice, never the criminal.

I've never felt anger like this before. I might combust.

I push past him and head straight for my room.

"Don't do this, Wren," he says. "It's not what you think. You don't know the whole story."

I can't speak. Tears pinch the backs of my eyes. My emotions rebel against me. Pain for the father I thought I had. Hands that I thought were holding me together were instead holding me back.

Chief tries to control himself. "I told you the pieces of the story I thought you could handle. Your mom left. She wasn't coming back. I didn't want to give you hope. It was better to give you a different story. I made the best choice I could at the time. That's what parents do. Right or wrong. It was more important for you to have the idea of a mother.

But not her. Not Vivienne. She would have disappointed you. I couldn't let that happen."

"You took us away from her," I say, barely above a whisper. The pain is worse like this—softly spoken words linger.

"If she wanted us, she wouldn't have done what she did," Chief replies steadily, though I see him cracking, breaking, sinking. But he pulls himself together, puts his hands on his hips—his move—like a police officer standing his ground. "Some mistakes have irreversible consequences. I promised myself I'd never put you in harm's way again."

But in leaving, he did. Chief ripped the hole. *He* is the reason for the scars left on my life by leaving. Not her.

From my closet I get the jar of pennies. I thought it was for Lizzie, but as it turns out, it's for me. Luca, Leia, and Baby Girl should be here soon. I start down the stairs, Chief following closely behind.

"You can't leave, Wren. You're only sixteen. You're a minor. I can have you tracked and back here within hours."

I stop, so completely resolved to what I need to do that a serene calm descends on me. No more tears. I've shed too many already.

"You knew where Lizzie went, and you didn't stop her. You let me suffer, wondering, and all this time, you knew."

"I thought she'd come back by now," he says. "And I didn't want to lose you, too."

"But in doing so, you did. Don't you understand?"

"You're my daughter," Chief insists, as if it's possible for that to change. He cracks, a tiny fissure right down the center of his chest. Sadness seeps out, midnight blue, flooding the room like water. "All I wanted to do was protect you."

"You know as well as I do, Chief. People in handcuffs always struggle to get free."

"*Please.* Please don't leave." He's desperate, but I can't stay. For once, I do the leaving.

Luca, Baby Girl, and Leia are waiting outside in Leia's truck. The day is cool. Clouds linger after last night's rain.

A yellow leaf dances in the street as I get in the truck.

Chief doesn't watch from the window as we pull away from the house. It seems to sink before my eyes, like a ship, the captain going down with it. Maybe I should have saved Chief, but we all make choices, and his drowned him long ago.

40

PALM TO PALM

The article I read on Luca's phone was from nearly fourteen years ago. It spoke about the sentencing of a woman charged with second-degree vehicular manslaughter and child abuse after she attempted to drive intoxicated the wrong way onto the highway and hit another car, killing the couple inside. Her two young children, ages four and two, were in the back seat. One suffered injuries—including a severely broken leg—and the other was unharmed.

Vivienne Rhine pleaded guilty and was sentenced to twelve years' imprisonment at the Pocatello Women's Correctional Center in Idaho.

She was released two years ago.

There is no looking back as Leia pulls onto the highway toward Boise. A flock of birds rises high into the sky, as if to guide us forward on our journey back home.

Rolling fields of amber wheat extend in front of us, the harvesting done, neat rows lining the land now, like waves. The vast swath of farmland known as the Palouse, south of Spokane, looks beautiful in the bright light of day. The gray of the city is gone. It's quiet out here. Life seems simpler without so many buildings. Just fields as far as we can see.

"Wreck Tangle," Leia says, her arm hanging out the window.

"I like that one," Baby Girl says, offering Leia a smile as she sits shotgun next to her.

"No," I say. "That doesn't feel like me."

"Belle on Wheels?" Luca offers. He's next to me in the somewhat cramped back seat of the truck.

"Gross. Too cute," Leia says from the driver's seat.

"But Wren *is* cute." Luca winks at me.

"Resident Shevil?" Baby Girl asks.

"Game Ovaries." Leia laughs.

Baby Girl adds, "Deathascope?"

"Wicked. I like that one," Leia says.

But my heart and my head aren't really into picking a Roller Derby name right now. I hug the jar of pennies closely.

"What are you going to do with those?" Leia asks.

"I don't know yet," I say. What does one do with freedom? There are choices to be made.

"You'll figure it out," Luca says.

A long silence hangs over the car. The sun streams in through the windshield. The wheat fields wave in the breeze.

"I'm scared," I say finally. At my confession, Luca takes my hand in his.

"It would be weird if you weren't," he says.

"It's going to be OK," Leia says. "No matter what happens, pain always fades with time."

"So do memories," Luca says. "Even the bad ones."

"Nothing lasts," Baby Girl says. She gives a knowing look at Leia, who reaches out and takes Baby Girl's hand in hers. Baby Girl told her everything, and it turns out Leia likes her more for it.

"Intoxiskate," Leia says.

"Skaterbrained," Baby Girl says.

I rest my head on Luca's shoulder and watch the world go by. "It really does look like amber waves."

"One day maybe we'll go to the ocean," he says, holding my hand. "But not today."

"I wish I could kiss you right now."

Luca and I lie in the bed of the truck, Leia and Baby Girl curled together inside, asleep. Overhead, clouds block the stars. Only tiny streaks of sunset sneak their way through to splatter color on the earth. We've made it to Boise, but my mom will have to wait until morning.

"You can kiss me," I say.

"No, because kissing will lead to other thoughts, and then I'll want to do those 'other thoughts' with you, and Leia's right there. I'm pretty sure she can kick my ass with one hand."

I have to hold back a giggle.

"I can wait to kiss you in the daylight," Luca says.

"You can?"

"My patience has grown this summer."

"It has?" I say skeptically.

"I'm like a monk now. I'm thinking about going into the seminary. My Catholic parents will be so proud."

"That's a terrible idea."

"Why?"

"No kissing allowed at seminary."

"Don't say the K-word." Luca bites his lip.

"OK," I say. "What about 'hug'? Can I say that?"

"Absolutely not."

"'Touch'?"

"Nooooo."

"'Snuggle'? 'Embrace'? 'Lips'?"

"You may need to stop talking. I'm not sure I can take it."

I turn toward him completely, rolling onto my hip and shoulder, my head resting on my arm.

"What about 'love'?" I whisper. "Can I say 'love'?"

Luca's dark hair matches the black clouds above us. His eyes are trained on me. "Only if you mean it."

I lean a little closer, forgetting air and space and rules, because now isn't the time to back away. It's the time to get close. Lean in. See. Be.

"Love," I say.

Our lips are just barely touching, so when he speaks, the word falls into my mouth, like a desperately needed drip of water.

"Love," he whispers.

We're still, our closeness like a protective shield.

"I think it's only right that you kiss me now," I say.

"Well, if I have to."

Luca brings his hand to my cheek and guides my lips to his. The kiss is simple, and I feel a sense of calm, of being, of stability I've never experienced before. The humble power of being in love and having that love returned. Whole. Holeless. One. There is no room for doubt to settle in, no crevices or wrinkles.

"I change my mind," Luca says. "I could never be a monk."

"Thank God." I smile, but it fades slightly. "What's going to happen?"

"What do you mean?"

I mean Utah. I mean my mom. I mean Chief and Lizzie and life.

"Only one thing is for certain," Luca says. "Tomorrow will eventually be a memory."

I lie back and look up at the stars.

"OK," I say. "Tomorrow's a memory."

And in the morning, when I wake up, our hands have crept toward each other and grabbed ahold, palm to palm, a simple kiss.

41

PRISON

What's my gesture?
    What's my punctuation?
    What's my vegetable?
    What's my color?
    What's my . . .
    What's my . . .
    What's my . . .

    Pat, I'd like to solve the puzzle.

    I am a songbird.
    And this is my song.
    Finally.

As she watched me paint a tree in her partially finished forest, Lizzie wanted to know about Monet.

"He painted with only nine colors," I said.

"Why only nine?" She examined the outline of a butterfly still dry-ing on her wall. "What about all the other colors? Why leave them out? Didn't he like them?"

"That's not how color works. I can make any color I want. All you need is a few, and you can paint a universe."

"Show me, Songbird."

Dabbing a little bit of yellow and red on my palm and swirling them together, I made orange.

"See?"

"Now my butterflies can be monarchs." Lizzie gasped. "You're magic, Songbird." She smiled and lay down on the floor, arms spread wide, an angel in a frozen forest. "This means we can make anything out of practically nothing."

"It's true."

"I have an idea," Lizzie said. "Let's paint her a life."

And so we did. We made a masterpiece out of stories we imagined.

All the fantasies Lizzie and I dreamed up for our mom ended the same.

"Maybe she's a Christian-radio host in North Dakota," Lizzie said. "Or a sound technician for Burning Man."

"Or an ocean photographer with over a million followers on Instagram."

"Or a tap-dancing street performer in New York."

"Or a CIA agent with a perfect Russian accent," I said, "living in Moscow and dining with Putin every night only to steal his secrets."

"Or the only midwife in a crumbling Syrian hospital, with bombs going off all around her. But she's vowed never to leave, because babies are born even in the middle of war and they deserve to be held lovingly when they take their first breath," Lizzie said. "She *has* to stay."

That's why she couldn't be with us.

In the name of love.

We may have come up with multiple versions of her story, but there was only one conclusion. One reason she lived without us.

We never imagined there could be a different ending.

Vivienne Rhine opens the front door of her cement-gray apartment, a cigarette oozing gray smoke between her fingers. She stares at me, knowingly. Like she expected that I'd show up and she's not too pleased about it.

"She said you would come." Vivienne pulls a drag from her cigarette. In all our imagining, she never smoked. Not in this addicted kind of way. The way that makes your face sour and your breath gross and your skin prematurely saggy. "She's been waiting for you."

Another drag, and a long exhale. Her hair is dyed black, with gray peeking out on the crown of her head. She is not the beautiful woman from the picture, with eyes the color of life. Premature death has settled into her features.

In some places, make-believe isn't possible.

She picks a piece of tobacco from her tongue and leans against the doorway.

"You came all this way and you're not going to speak?"

What is there to say? For years I imagined a woman, but not her. And in all my fantasies, we never spoke. There was more magic in silence.

Where is the woman Chief loves?

"Your sister wanted me to give you something." Vivienne walks into her apartment, letting the door close slightly, as if to tell me to stay put, and returns a moment later with a book. She hands it to me.

When Instinct Goes Wrong: An Investigation of Woodpeckers and Their Relationship with Wood.

"Kind of an odd book," Vivienne says.

"I'm kind of an odd person." I run my hand over the cover. Lizzie had it all this time. I open to the page where my secret has hidden for years, but a postcard has been placed there instead.

Self-Portrait with a Beret, 1886	

Dear Songbird,
  "Everyone discusses my art and pretends to understand, as if it were necessary to understand, when it is simply necessary to love." —Claude Monet
  I love you,
  Lizzie
	Wren Plumley
	20080 21st Ave.
	Spokane, WA 99203

This one is handwritten in Lizzie's circular scrawl, like all the postcards she sent when I was younger, when she was pretending to be the woman who now stands before me. I don't know which I prefer—Lizzie's smooth handwriting or the reality—but I'm not sure it's necessary to know.

"That's Monet, right?" Vivienne says, pointing to the picture on the front. She pulls another drag from her cigarette. It's down to just a nub now.

I nod.

"Look, I told your dad years ago that I wasn't fit to be a mom. That hasn't changed. I don't know what you girls want from me."

"Nothing," I say, examining the gray walls and the gray smoke and Vivienne's gray aura. A person doesn't have to be behind bars to be in a prison.

We all decide when it's time to let ourselves out. To be free.

And I didn't come here for her.

Before I leave for good, I say, "When you see Lizzie again, tell her she can come home now."

42

BACK WHERE YOU BELONG

I walk up to the reception desk at the Spokane Public Library.

"I'm here to return a book."

I hand the librarian the copy of *When Instinct Goes Wrong: An Investigation of Woodpeckers and Their Relationship with Wood.* She scans it.

"We've been waiting for this to be returned," she says.

"Me, too."

She goes to set it among the pile of books for reshelving.

"Do you mind if I put it back?" I ask her. "I know exactly where it goes."

"Are you sure?"

"Positive. I'll make sure it doesn't go missing again."

On the fifth floor, among the stacks of research papers and old encyclopedias, secrets are tucked between pages of facts. For so long I wanted to find Lizzie's truth, but what I discovered was my own.

This was never about her. Even she knew that.

It's the story of a songbird.

Only one more secret belongs here. And then it's done.

So do woodpeckers get headaches or what? I imagine Wilder asking.

"I'm not sure it matters," I whisper aloud. "They're still going to peck wood. It's in their nature. I think it's time we just let it be."

Wilder is a memory now, but even so, I can almost hear him saying, *Birds will be birds.*

On a lone piece of paper, I write my secret about a boy with constellation freckles and red hair, who flipped on a light in the darkness and turned my life upside down. I place it between two pages and close the book. Done.

"Birds will be birds," I say, and walk away.

Alone.

43

FREEDOM

It's the middle of the night. Rosario's Market is closed. The lights are off inside. I hold the jar of pennies. Thousands of them. Each one stored for just the right time. Saved for Lizzie, but meant for me. Freedom in a jar.

Leia, Baby Girl, Luca, and I stare at the mechanical horse.

"Do you regret it?" Leia asks. "Seeing your mom?"

"No," I say. "I needed to know."

"It's the same way I feel about Doritos. Am I bummed I can never eat them again? Sure. But is it more important I don't poison myself with shit that's going to give me cancer? Yes."

"A profound statement, Princess," Luca says.

"Food is totally a metaphor for life," she says. "Just because it tastes good doesn't mean you should eat it. As much as it sucks, it's better to eat your broccoli most days."

"The truth is broccoli," Baby Girl proclaims. "It smells, tastes even worse, but it keeps the heart healthy."

"I like my heart," I say with a quick glance at Luca. "It's more reliable than my head."

"The only junk food I'm eating from this day forward is marshmallows. One in particular," he says. "That's all I need."

"So who wants the first ride?" I ask, shaking the jar.

"That's a lot of pennies," Leia says. "I hope there's time."

"You, Wren," Baby Girl says. "You do it. Show us how it's done."

So I climb onto the horse, drop a penny into the machine, and wait. And wait. And wait. Leia inspects the horse. She shakes it once.

"I think freedom's broken," Luca says.

"How apropos," Leia says.

"That's OK," Baby Girl says. "A wise person once said, 'You can't *do* freedom. You have to *be* it.'"

"Genius," Leia says. "Who said that?"

Baby Girl smiles at me. "Wren."

"Well, what do we do now?" Luca asks.

I set the jar of pennies next to the horse. "I guess we'll just have to wait for the horse to be fixed."

"That might take a while," Leia says. "There's a lot broken in this world."

"That's OK," I say. "We're not going anywhere."

We all take a seat on the curb, a mini-rainbow of auras—turquoise, orchid, cadmium yellow, and shamrock green. Maybe Monet saw auras, too. Maybe he collected nine colors because each one meant something special to him.

"I figured it out," I say. "My roller-girl name."

"I'm proud of you," Leia says.

"I'm glad one of us knows who we are," Baby Girl says.

"You'll get there," Leia says. "We'll all get there."

"But maybe just not tonight. We can blame it on the broken horse." Luca grins, and the dark lights up with sunlight. "So what's the name, Wren? Who are you?"

Who am I? The answer comes easily now.

And I say, "Plum Crazy."

44

HOW IT ENDS

When life isn't working, take another perspective. That's what Chief and I are trying to do. It's how to move on.

"Before and After," he says. He's on the couch in the living room, drinking chamomile tea to help him sleep. Leia convinced him it would be better for his health than beer.

I know why Chief has deep wrinkles around his eyes that crinkle and crease, even when he's resting. I know why he holds on tightly, why he lives in the dark and fights the lurking shadows when other people are sleeping.

He told me the story. How love lives in the cracks and the crevices and the wrinkles. He finally let me dig down and pull it out of him.

He told me how he met a woman who bent light and shifted his world and made living feel effervescent. How he wanted her for all eternity, but she was haunted by a darkness even Chief couldn't tame. So he gave her light the only way he knew how—two baby girls.

"You and Lizzie," Chief said. "I thought it would solve our problems, but it wasn't that easy."

When a call came in to the Boise Police Department about a car crash near Interstate 84, he was the first person to the scene of the accident.

"When I heard the make of the car and license plate, I was paralyzed," he said. "And then I heard two deceased. It took me five minutes to get there. For five minutes I thought you and Lizzie were dead."

Chief shuddered, tears in his eyes, and any anger I had seemed small then next to what he experienced. Next to death.

"It wasn't right to be relieved—two people died that day—but by God, I was."

Vivienne was drunk and high on pain pills. Chief blamed himself. He knew she was struggling with depression and addiction, but he thought if he loved her hard enough, it would go away.

"Two people died because of me," he said. "It's my job to serve and protect, and I let my own blindness cloud my judgment. I couldn't stay in that town. And your mom . . . It was like she wanted to go to jail. She wanted out of our life together."

It was then that I understood: Chief didn't completely lie to me and Lizzie. Our mom *did* leave, just not how we thought.

I see him differently now, all the intricate parts that make Chief who he is—the strings that weave his story.

"Horse ranch dressing!" he yells at the TV.

"Dude ranch dressing," I correct him, my roller skates in hand. "You're kind of terrible at this game, Chief."

He doesn't get offended. The glory of the win isn't why he plays. Chief just wants to spend time with me.

"Derby practice?" he asks.

"Yeah, I'm meeting my friends at the high school."

"Will *Luca* be there?" he asks in a mock-swoony voice.

I roll my eyes at him. I'm starting to think maybe that's my gesture. Or maybe . . . it doesn't matter.

"None of your business," I say.

Luca convinced his parents that Catholic school isn't for him and that if he enrolls in public school, he might actually go. They said yes, and he starts at South Hill High in a few weeks. I told him about Chloe and how she's Anne Boleyn and Jay is Henry VIII and I'm still a nobody.

Luca said, "Nobodies to some are somebodies to others."

Roller Derby starts next week. I'm nervous and scared, but Baby Girl promises she'll be there to cheer me on. She quit her job at the carousel.

"Time for a new song," she said.

Leia got her a job at Rosario's Market, so now they get to spend more time together.

Chief had the cruiser returned to the driveway, and Olga's back. He apologized and rehired her. She's started cooking dinner for us. When she is in the kitchen, spatula in hand, Chief standing nearby with a cup of tea, it dawns on me that maybe we were a complete family all along.

A new puzzle appears on the screen, Vanna gesturing to the unknown letters. Chief sits relaxed on the couch, sunlight streaming through the windows.

"Remember when I said I thought something was going on next door?" Chief says. "Turns out I was right."

I lace up my roller skates. "Really?"

"The house finally sold," he says. He blows on the top of his tea. "That place has been vacant for so long, I was worried it would never sell."

"Things change," I say.

"Yes, they do."

A contestant spins the wheel and guesses the letter *T*.

Pat says, "There are three *T*s." The audience claps.

"Wren?" Chief says in a serious tone.

"Yeah, Chief?"

But he softens. "Have fun."

Luca and I sit at the bus stop to nowhere.

"How about Paris?" he says. "We could go see Monet's house."

"We don't know how to speak French."

"True. I do know how to do *something* French, though."

He kisses me, and my insides melt.

"OK, Paris is out," Luca says when our lips finally separate. "London?"

"What if we're not back in time for homecoming? I've never been to a dance before."

"And my parents throw a really good Christmas party. You can't miss it."

"And what if the Seahawks make it to the Super Bowl? Chief will make his tuna casserole. If we're gone, he'll have no one to help him not eat it."

"Sounds delicious."

"And then it'll be spring," I say.

"And the lilacs will bloom."

"We can't miss that."

"No," Luca says. "We can't."

We take a breath and sit back, waiting for a bus that will never come.

"I guess we'll have to stay right here," he says.

"Together."

"Together."

I lie on the ground in Lizzie's room, my shamrock-green aura mingling with all the other colors of the forest. I was here all along. I just couldn't see it.

My story starts with a single tree, painted on a wall, and it grows from there.

Aren't memories just made-up stories that we tell ourselves, anyway? We dictate what we see and how we want to remember.

Sometimes that's what we need to do to get by, to get through, to move on. To find what's real.

But stories must come to an end.

"Hey, Songbird," Lizzie says. "Time to paint me a new story."

ACKNOWLEDGMENTS

Let me take a moment to acknowledge the people who help to make my life of creativity and imagination possible.

Jason Kirk, my editor extraordinaire: You always know what my work needs. Thank you for polishing and pruning my stories and for constantly saying, "Yes and . . ." even when I come to you with an idea to write a book about a girl named after a bird and her imaginary friend. You encourage me to be bold with my work. That is a gift and one I'm so grateful to receive.

A huge thank-you to Coco Williams. Not only do you check my text messages for teen accuracy, but without you I'm pretty sure my publishing career would not be nearly as bright. You are a light. Shine on.

Renee Nyen, my agent and friend: From what this book was to what it is now, you've been there for the journey. Wren and Wilder thank you and so do I.

Kyle Crane, my beloved: From your very logical ideas on solving my creative blocks, to the moments of quiet when you just let my mind be the whirling dervish that it is, and to all the spaces in between, I love you. I'm your biggest fan. Let's keep traveling the world together.

To the people who light up my life—Drew, Hazel, Mom, Dad, Anna, Emmy, my friends and family near and far—thank you for painting the canvas of my life.

And again, to the readers, for whom this book is dedicated. It is for you. Always and forever. You are my sunshine.

ABOUT THE AUTHOR

Photo © 2018 Kate Testerman Photography

Rebekah Crane is the author of several critically acclaimed young-adult novels, including *The Infinite Pieces of Us*, *The Upside of Falling Down*, *The Odds of Loving Grover Cleveland*, *Aspen* (currently being adapted by Life Out Loud Films), and *Playing Nice*. Crane is a former high school English teacher who found a passion for writing young-adult fiction while studying secondary English education at Ohio University.

After living and teaching in six different cities, Crane finally settled in the foothills of the Rocky Mountains to write novels and work on screenplays. A yoga instructor and the mother of two girls, Crane spends many of her days tucked behind a laptop at 7,500 feet, where the altitude only enhances the writing experience. Visit www.rebekahcrane.com, follow her on Twitter, or like her on Facebook at authorrebekahcrane.